MW01132125

Never Look Back

Paranormal Huntress Series, Volume 1

W.J. May

Published by Dark Shadow Publishing, 2017.

This is a work of fiction. Similarities to real people, places, or events are entirely coincidental.

NEVER LOOK BACK

First edition. June 2, 2017.

Copyright © 2017 W.J. May.

Written by W.J. May.

Also by W.J. May

Bit-Lit Series
Lost Vampire
Cost of Blood
Price of Death

Blood Red Series
Courage Runs Red
The Night Watch
Marked by Courage
Forever Night
The Other Side of Fear
Blood Red Box Set Books #1-5

Daughters of Darkness: Victoria's Journey
Victoria
Huntress
Coveted (A Vampire & Paranormal Romance)
Twisted
Daughter of Darkness - Victoria - Box Set

Great Temptation Series
The Devil's Footsteps
Heaven's Command
Mortals Surrender

Hidden Secrets Saga
Seventh Mark - Part 1
Seventh Mark - Part 2
Marked By Destiny
Compelled
Fate's Intervention
Chosen Three
The Hidden Secrets Saga: The Complete Series

Kerrigan Chronicles
Stopping Time
A Passage of Time
Ticking Clock
Secrets in Time
Time in the City
Ultimate Future
Guilt Of My Past

Mending Magic Series
Lost Souls
Illusion of Power

Challenging the Dark
Castle of Power
Limits of Magic
Protectors of Light

Omega Queen Series
Discipline
Bravery
Courage
Conquer
Strength
Validation
Approval
Blessing

Paranormal Huntress Series
Never Look Back
Coven Master
Alpha's Permission
Blood Bonding
Oracle of Nightmares
Shadows in the Night
Paranormal Huntress BOX SET

Prophecy Series
Only the Beginning
White Winter
Secrets of Destiny

The Chronicles of Kerrigan: Gabriel
Living in the Past
Present For Today
Staring at the Future

The Chronicles of Kerrigan Prequel
Christmas Before the Magic
Question the Darkness
Into the Darkness
Fight the Darkness
Alone in the Darkness
Lost in Darkness
The Chronicles of Kerrigan Prequel Series Books #1-3

The Chronicles of Kerrigan Sequel
A Matter of Time
Time Piece
Second Chance
Glitch in Time
Our Time
Precious Time

The Hidden Secrets Saga
Seventh Mark (part 1 & 2)

Nonsense

Perception

The Senseless - Box Set Books #1-4

Standalone

Shadow of Doubt (Part 1 & 2)

Five Shades of Fantasy

Zwarte Nevel

Shadow of Doubt - Part 1

Shadow of Doubt - Part 2

Four and a Half Shades of Fantasy

Dream Fighter

What Creeps in the Night

Forest of the Forbidden

Arcane Forest: A Fantasy Anthology

The First Fantasy Box Set

Watch for more at www.wjmaybooks.com.

Paranormal Huntress Series #1

Never Look Back

By W.J. May

Copyright 2017 by W.J. May

Paranormal Huntress Series

Find W.J. May

Website:
http://www.wanitamay.yolasite.com
Facebook:
https://www.facebook.com/pages/Author-WJ-May-FAN-PAGE/
141170442608149
Newsletter:
SIGN UP FOR W.J. May's Newsletter to find out about new releases, updates, cover reveals and even freebies!
http://eepurl.com/97aYf

NEVER LOOK BACK - Blurb:

The wise learn many things from their enemies.

MY NAME'S ATLANTA SKOLAR, and I'm a huntress. No, not the vampire-slaying type, or like the ever-brooding Winchester brothers from *Supernatural*. I live a relatively normal life—during the day at least. I go to school, have friends, and try my best to survive Uncle James' horrendous cooking.

However, the nights in the city of Calen are not always calm. There's a thin veil between our world and the world of monsters, the good and the bad. I'm one of the few who stands between the two. With the help of my uncle, who's taken me in since my parents' deaths, I spend the nights making sure the balance is maintained and that each side keeps to their respective places.

At least, that was until something rattled the cages and everything hit the fan. There's a new evil in town, an evil that's been here before, and it may be responsible for my parents' deaths. An evil that isn't satisfied with the balance. It'll do all it can to make sure darkness falls over Calen and the rest of the world once again.

Scary? That ain't the half of it.

It's particularly interested in me.

Why? No idea.

But it's my job as a huntress to make sure the evil is stopped, no matter what.

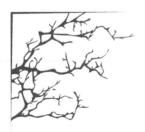

Chapter 1

LOUIS SPRINTED THROUGH the darkness.

His feet echoed against the alleyway walls, droplets of water splattering up as he dashed through puddles that had remained since the rain from the night before. A strong wind blew against him and hit at the flaps of his coat, forcing an unwanted resistance to his run. His breath escaped in gasps of white vapor.

He ventured a look behind him, and his eyes widened as he saw how close his pursuer was. Louis quickened his pace, pushing himself harder. His legs burned in protest as he jumped over garbage cans and kicked through cardboard boxes.

He needed to get out into the open, and quickly.

Claws scratched at his back, and he felt the deep sting of fresh gouges against the fabric of his shirt. The pain only pushed him harder, and despite the ever-nearing mouth of the alleyway Louis knew he wouldn't make it out alive. He threw caution to the wind, drawing on the little bit of strength he had left, and made for the nearest wall. He jumped, his feet skidding slightly against the wet asphalt, and flung forward. As soon as he was on the wall he raced upwards on his hands and feet, scaling the building with ease.

His pursuer gave chase.

Louis could feel the dampness from last night's downpour on the cold bricks, but that wasn't what caused him to shiver. He could hear the grunting of his pursuer behind him; growling pants as the man, who'd been chasing him for the past half hour, relentlessly followed. Louis weighed his options quickly, his mind racing with possible solutions, but his fear made it impossible for him to grasp onto a single strand of logic. All he had was his fight or flight instincts, and right now they were telling him to run faster.

Once on the roof, Louis swiftly landed on his feet and continued forward, dashing across the building. There was no escape, and he couldn't risk jumping off towards the street. It had taken his race generations to maintain their secrecy, and he wasn't about to ruin that. He could only hope that his pursuer would eventually tire and allow Louis to outrun him.

Louis dashed for the far end of the rooftop, and his eyes made a quick calculation of the distance between this one and the neighboring building. He could scale it easily, he knew that, but the real question was what then? He could almost feel the hot breath of his pursuer on the back of his neck, and despite everything Louis had tried it seemed like only he was tiring.

He frowned, bared his fangs, and pushed harder just as the skies above him burst in a clash of thunder and bright flashes of lightning. He reached the end of the roof, pushed against the surface, and took off. He felt the wind blow against him, the first drops of rain falling like slow motion, and the sharp clasp of a claw around his ankle.

Pulled back forcefully, he was tossed to the side like a rag doll. His head hit the roof and he could almost hear the bone cracking, his vision bursting into flashes of colors as he stumbled and rolled. But if there was one thing Louis Lesoleil was known for it was his speed, and he instantly pushed himself onto his feet.

The hand which had grabbed him wrapped around his neck and pressed hard, breaking Louis' retreat and forcing him to gasp. The tension was strong, squeezing and blocking his airway, and Louis lashed out wildly as the hand lifted him up off his feet easily.

"This is the end of the line, Louis," a voice hissed behind him, and Louis growled as the hand brought him down quickly and slammed him into the roof.

Louis cried out as the bones in his nose cracked and blood spurted out in bursts of dark red. He turned over slowly, his vision blurry, the cloaked man standing over him a menacing presence. The clouds floodgates had opened completely, and the rain fell in torrents around them. From underneath the cloak's hood, twin eyes burned a bright red, and a mouth opened to rows of fanged teeth.

The figure's entire face seemed to shift in and out focus. Louis could hardly believe what he was gazing at. "Impossible!" Louis coughed. "You can't be here! None of you can! We closed the door!"

The hooded figure's mouth widened in a terrible grin. "Times have changed," came a voice akin to nails scratching across a blackboard. "The shift in power begins now!"

Louis sat up slowly. Just as he was about to reply, he gasped as the hooded figure's hand burst through his chest and the clawed hand wrapped around his heart. He instinctively grabbed the arm buried inside him and tried to pull it away, his eyes locked onto the burning flames staring back at him.

The hooded figure snickered and squeezed as Louis' cries echoed in the night.

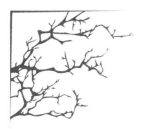

Chapter 2

ATLANTA SAT UP IN BED with a start.

She fought to control her breathing, her head turning from side to side as her blurry vision still played parts of the nightmare. For a split second, she could still feel the walls closing in around her; the claustrophobia smothering her, dark fumes from a fire filling her nose with the wretched stench of burning bodies.

And in it all, eyes. Red eyes. Staring at her.

You're okay. You're okay.

She gasped and forced her breathing to slow, fighting desperately for control. The walls around her slowly moved back to their regular places, and the shrill sound of her alarm clock made her jump. She pressed a hand against her chest, as if willing the thumping there to slow down, and winced at the pain her fast-beating heart was causing. She sniffed, inhaled and exhaled slowly, and shook her head as she tried to rid her nostrils of the smell of burning.

It's not a dream. Something's actually burning.

Atlanta quickly slammed her hand against the alarm and scurried out bed, her sweat-soaked blanket tossed to one side as her feet touched the cold wooden floor of her bedroom. She quickly glanced at her window quickly, taking in the orange beams of light escaping through her curtains, and pulled her t-shirt on.

Out her room and on the second-floor landing, the smell of burning grew stronger now. "Hello?" she called out, descending the stairs by twos and bracing herself against the possibility of a fire. "Uncle James!"

"In here!" came the almost childlike reply from the kitchen, the hoarse voice of her uncle mixed with curses and chuckles as pans clanged against each other.

Atlanta raced across the hallway and into the kitchen, her nose wrinkling as the source of the smell made itself visible. Her uncle stood at the far end of the kitchen, racing back and forth between the sink and stove as black smoke rose from one of the pans there. She watched him grab the pan, and cringed when he hollered in pain.

She hurried towards the stove, grabbing one of the mitts off the kitchen table, and with a quick flick of her hand turned the stove off and launched the pan into the sink. She turned the faucet on and stepped back as the water hissed against the scalding pan and whatever it was her uncle was trying to cook in it.

"So much for breakfast." Uncle James chuckled, shaking his singed hand. "That was supposed to be French toast."

"One day you're going to burn the house down!" Atlanta sighed, grabbing her uncle's hand and inspecting the burns. When she was satisfied that it wasn't serious, she sighed heavily and shook her head at him. "Didn't we say you'd leaving the cooking to me?"

Uncle James laughed, his burly figure shaking with merriment and his shoulders bouncing up and down. "I couldn't help myself," he said with a grin. "One day you're going to realize I'm not as bad as you think."

Atlanta smiled despite herself. "One day?" She raised an eyebrow at him. "Just make sure we're out in the open when that happens. I kinda like this house."

James Skolar clapped her on the shoulder with his burnt hand and immediately winced, breaking from a chuckle to a moan. He set himself down on one of the kitchen chairs and rifled through the pages of a cookbook he'd left open there, then closed it and tossed it into the garbage.

Atlanta watched in amusement, quickly tying her bright blonde hair into a ponytail with the elastic hairband she had around her wrist at all times. "I didn't hear you come in last night," she said, opening a cupboard and pulling out the cereal. *Breakfast of champions*, she thought to herself.

"Actually, I just got in," James replied, stifling a sudden yawn.

Atlanta set two bowls on the table and pushed the milk towards her uncle, only now noticing he was still wearing his jeans and shirt. "How was the funeral?"

"Depressing," James replied, nodding as he took the box of cereal from her and filled his bowl. "Dark. And dangerous."

Atlanta nodded as she poured herself a bowl and sat down. The news of Louis Lesoleil's murder travelled quickly, and even though she'd wanted to go to the funeral as well her uncle had advised against it. Besides, the last time she had been to the Fortress, it hadn't ended in the best of ways.

"Marcus is obviously devastated," James broke through her thoughts. "The Vamps are out for blood, that's for sure."

"Do they know who did it?" she asked, stuffing the first spoonful of cereal into her mouth and glancing up at the clock on the wall. She didn't want to be late for school.

"Claws, scratches, fist through the heart," James sighed. "All points to the Pack."

"That doesn't make sense," Atlanta said, frowning. "There's been peace between the two families for centuries. Why break that now?"

James shook his head and shrugged, pushing his untouched breakfast to the side. "There's going to be a meeting tonight," he said, slowly pushing himself out of his chair. "You get to school and worry about your tests. Leave the families to me." He ruffled her hair and walked out of the kitchen.

She absently finished her cereal and made her way back up to her bedroom. Her mind raced with flashes of her nightmare, a mix of fire and screams lingering in the back of her head like a bad headache. She could hear her uncle snoring from his own bedroom, the usual sign that he was more than exhausted, and she chuckled to herself.

Ever since her parents' death, Uncle James was all the family she had. She didn't know anything else, and she owed him so much. She could only imagine what it had been like for him, being handed the responsibility of a two-year-old girl, expected to raise her in a world that was far from kind. Personally, she thought he had done a great job so far...despite the frequent burnt dinners.

She sorted through her clothes, picking out the most comfortable ensemble she could find, and quickly got dressed. Barefoot, she dashed about her room, packing her bag and making sure she hadn't left any of her due assignments behind. Her cellphone rang just as she was leaving her bedroom, and Skylar's name flashed on the screen.

"Two minutes," Atlanta said upon answering, dropping to her knees and pulling a chest out from under her bed.

"I never get how you wake up at dawn every morning," Skylar chastised, "and still manage to keep me waiting."

Atlanta sighed and opened the chest. "I said two minutes, Skylar," she said, gazing at the various weapons inside before opting for a black-hilted knife with golden symbols etched into it. It had been her first weapon, a present from her Uncle James on her twelfth birthday when he had turned her world upside down. She remembered hating him for it back then, but now she had a completely different respect for the man. She could only imagine how difficult it must have been for him.

"Fine," Skylar sighed in frustration, "but if I miss watching Ryan Toller walk down the hallway this morning, I'm going to hate you forever."

Atlanta hung up with a smile. She reached for a sheath, wrapped it around her forearm, and slid the knife into place. Grabbing her coat, she made sure the long sleeves of her shirt concealed the weapon, and raced downstairs.

If Louis Lesoleil's murder was going to cause ripples, then Calen High was going to be very interesting today.

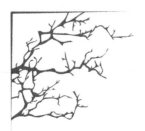

Chapter 3

CALEN WAS A CITY THAT had very little to offer.

Much like any other metropolis, it wasn't known for its charm or hospitality. The people weren't welcoming, and it was commonplace to find yourself in the middle of a brawl that broke out for absolutely no reason. Traffic sucked; public transportation sucked, too. It was a loud and dark city; its skyscrapers towering over the ghettos a stark reminder that, even here, the rich got richer and the poor grew poorer.

Still, for many it was home, and Atlanta couldn't imagine living anywhere else. Despite being raised in the suburbs the city was still hers, and she had long since decided that she would live and die here. Besides, although Calen was not known for being the center of anything, it was definitely the heart and soul of her world. The underworld. The world between the cracks that very few people ventured into and ever came back from in one piece.

Sitting in the passenger seat beside Skylar, her blonde friend chatting about random things Atlanta had quickly learned to filter, she gazed out the window at the passing houses. One of the calmer neighborhoods of Calen's suburbs, Witch Hills, appeared to be a little more upscale and detached from the hustle and bustle of downtown. The ubiquitous gothic architecture throughout the city seemed a little Gotham-Batman style, but was still a signature trait of Calen and everything it stood for.

She remembered the first time Uncle James had told her the truth about the city. She could still feel the sting of tears in her eyes as he filled her in on the details of what actually made Calen breathe. Vampires, Werewolves, Wizards, and Witches. The whole gamut of monsters and ghouls that lurked in the darkest of corners; just out sight, yet there. The city may not have been a tourist trap, but it was the home to more than just wealthy businessmen and struggling youth.

"Are you even listening to me?"

Atlanta turned and looked at the frown on Skylar's face, the other girl's eyes snapping back and forth between Atlanta and the road.

Atlanta gave her a quick smile and nodded. Skylar could be a monster herself when she felt she was being ignored.

"Really?" Skylar clicked her tongue. "What was the last thing I said?"

"That you weren't going to take no for an answer," Atlanta replied immediately.

Skylar gazed at her for a moment before returning her attention to the road and sighing heavily. "Sometimes I wonder where you go when you drift off like that."

"Nowhere in particular," she said, looking back out the window. The drive to school consisted of Skylar doing all the talking and Atlanta listening, a ritual that helped clear her mind and ease into the world of regular people. They were only ten minutes away from school, and today wasn't one of those days Atlanta wanted to change that.

Her mind was still playing images from her nightmare. For the past week, it had been the same. She stood trapped in a room, the world around her burning and the walls crumbling around her. In the distance, between the smoke and flames, red eyes stared at her and a manic laugh seemed to echo in the crackling of the fire. And every morning she would wake up sweaty, with a feeling of impending death that had grown suffocating.

Adding to the bad dream, Louis' murder didn't rest easy on her mind. She knew the man well, her closest ally in the circle of the Fortress, one of the very few Vamps who didn't automatically want to rip her to shreds the moment he saw her. Centuries old but looking not a day over eighteen, it was sometimes hard to believe Louis had been one of the most important leaders in the vampire family. His murder was definitely a blow to the Vamps in general.

And obviously to Marcus. The leader of the family was not one to anger. It was absurd that someone would be as bold as to kill the man's only living relative—well, as living as a vampire could be.

"Girl, you're throwing me off my game." Skylar shook her head as she pulled into the high school parking lot. Finding herself a comfortable slot near the east end, she jerked the car to a halt.

Atlanta shot her a glare and both girls laughed. They got out, backpacks slung over their shoulders, and subconsciously Atlanta brushed her hand against the concealed knife. She hoped she wouldn't need it today, but there was no telling what the response would be from the Vamps. Marcus wouldn't risk disturbing the peace, especially after all this time, but some of the younger, more volatile vampires were dangerously unpredictable.

Atlanta kept close to Skylar, eyeing the other students filing towards the majestic school. The massive structure had been standing since the nineteenth century, built as a castle for an unknown king who never lasted. Its massive walls, gothic towers, and lines of frozen gargoyles were certainly enough to make anyone stop and stare, or believe in mythical creatures.

Atlanta knew the truth. The Druids had built it, once housing hundreds of the magical men and women and their extensive knowledge. It had always been the center of the darker world of Calen, where peace between the warring families had finally been cemented and laws were established to maintain it. It was where the Hand had been forged to maintain that peace, Druids-turned-warriors insistent on making sure each family kept to its word, and every monster respected the laws.

It was a symbol of unity, but to the rest of the world it was just a massive educational center where bullies still stuffed heads into toilet seats, the lonely sought affection from the cheerleaders and jocks, and standardized testing ruled students' lives. It angered Atlanta sometimes, but she'd learned to accept what was necessary to make sure the balance between both worlds was maintained.

"Hurry up," Skylar urged, grabbing Atlanta by the arm and pulling her along. "I don't want to miss Ryan!"

Atlanta smiled as they half-jogged towards the building, pushing through half-sleeping students trudging up the massive steps like zombies, and entered the school's large lobby. All around them, the sounds of chatter and laughter mixed with the metallic opening and slamming of lockers, and Atlanta let her friend guide her deeper into the school.

She waved at a couple of her friends, but there was no stopping Skylar as she dragged her to their lockers.

"Here he comes," Skylar chirped.

Atlanta turned to where her friend was looking. Ryan Toller was probably the most eminent student in Calen High. Quarterback of the Calen Wizards, ripped to perfection, and with a head of thick black hair above deep green eyes, he had all the high school students of the city drooling over him. Every morning Skylar had them watch him stroll down the hallway towards his first class as he flashed smiles that made most girls swoon, high-fived teammates, and generally acted like a celebrity walking down the red carpet. Atlanta often joked that all he needed were flashing lights and cameras. It never made Skylar laugh.

Ryan walked past them, giving Skylar a wink and a small smile, his eyes briefly meeting Atlanta's before turning away. It was all Atlanta needed to see the uneasiness there, and before she could turn back to her locker and ready herself for her first class Ryan stopped. He turned around and walked up to her, easily a foot taller than her, and looked at her seriously.

"I'm sorry about Louis," Ryan said, his voice low.

Atlanta nodded quickly, trying her best not to appear uncomfortable. She could feel Skylar's eyes boring into her.

"If there's anything—"

"Not now," Atlanta cut him off.

Ryan looked at her for a beat, then nodded and continued on his way, easing back into his confident, celebrity-like stride.

Skylar stepped in close, her face flushed and eyes wide. "What was *that* about? He *knows* you?"

"His father knows my uncle," Atlanta said dismissively and opened her locker.

"Who's Louis?"

"No one," Atlanta lied. "It doesn't matter." She hated lying to Skylar, and a part of her fumed that Ryan had approached her like that in public. There were rules to these things, and breaking them brought unnecessary attention and caused unwanted problems. She could already feel the myriad in questions in Skylar's mind, questions she would be forced to answer one way or the other because her friend never let go of anything, and her mind raced with possible answers that would sound logical.

Besides, there was no way Atlanta could explain that Ryan Toller was the eldest son of the Werewolf family and heir to the Pack.

Chapter 4

JAMES SKOLAR COULD feel the heaviness in the air around him.

He sat poignantly at the elongated table smack in the center of the Dome. On either side of the table, each occupying their own seat and flanked by the best of their guards, sat the heads of the Vampire and Werewolf families. James could feel the tension in the air, the visible restraint each man fought to maintain in the face of the recent tragedy. He wrapped his hands around the staff lying softly on his lap, his fingers tracing the symbols etched into the wood, and prayed things would not escalate.

Over the past few decades, the Dome had become neutral ground where the two families could meet and discuss the most important issues at hand. Usually, these meetings were quite civil. Vampires and werewolves setting their differences aside as they focused on one problem or the other. Ever since the Insurgence almost a century before, the families knew that their combined strength was all that assured their continued existence in this world.

"*I* will not be as bold as to blame your family for this atrocity," Marcus spoke up suddenly, his voice echoing off the stone walls and filling every crevice of the Dome.

James glanced up in surprise. He'd always admired the man's power and authority, as well as the poised dignity with which he carried himself. Alive since the fall of Rome, Marcus was among the very few vampires who had crossed the ocean and settled successfully in the New World. James remembered the history well—how Marcus had survived the mass hunt against his kind, the last remaining vampire of the original Circle that had made the long voyage west.

When it came to this side of the ocean there was no denying who was in charge, and Marcus' power oozed out of him like a heavy veil.

"I appreciate your faith, Marcus," came the reply from the other end of the table. "I assure you, we are not to blame for something as cowardly as this."

James looked over to his old friend. What Colin Toller lacked in century-old wisdom, he made up for in brute strength and size. Ever since they'd been in high school together, the head of the Calen Pack had always looked like he could lift an entire bus in one hand while breaking a man in half with the other. His pack was the most loyal of the four Packs, and his authority over Calen and its surrounding area—a dominion his ancestors had ruled for centuries—was unprecedented. Although their lives had taken them in different directions, neither man forgot how important their bond was.

"There is, however, the matter of retribution," Marcus said softly, his voice seeping from between his lips in a soothing, yet dangerous, tone. "Something like this cannot go unpunished."

Colin nodded, his eyes fixated on the other man. "We're doing everything we can to make sure we find who did this."

A smile formed on Marcus' lips, a terrible smile that lacked any kind of joviality. "I believe that won't be enough, Colin," he said. "There are those in my family who have been greatly affected by this transgression. Those who long for justice, and are not afraid to seek it for themselves."

James' head snapped towards the vampire, and he instantly felt the heavy surge of rage escaping from Colin.

"I'm confident that your authority over all is supreme," Colin remarked between clenched teeth. "I cannot believe anyone would step out of line without your blessing."

Marcus leaned back in his seat and eyed Colin with amusement. Before, it had been easy to prompt an outburst from Colin. A few words here, a gesture there, and the hot-blooded Werewolf would instantly burst into rage. Now, though, Colin seemed to be a lot more in control, no doubt a trait his father had beat into him well before handing over power. In the past twenty years alone, Marcus was never disappointed with how much Colin continued to surprise him.

"That's true," Marcus replied. "But for how long? You can only keep a fire controlled for so long before it burns out of control."

"I wouldn't know," Colin responded, smiling, trying his best to control his anger. "But, then again, I haven't been around as long as you have. I'd like to think one learns much over the years, and you, Marcus, have had centuries to learn."

"Do not presume to understand me, pup," Marcus hissed.

"Do not threaten me again, fangs," Colin spat back.

Marcus stood suddenly and slammed his fists onto the stone table, the sound of his onslaught booming through the Dome. His guards immediately bared their fangs, and on the other end of the table the wolves began to shift.

"Gentlemen!" James shouted, bringing out his staff and slamming its tip on the floor. The symbols etched across it burst into bright orange colors, and both leaders instantly gazed at him in a mix of anger and fear. It took them a while, but eventually both men sat back in their seats.

"We're here to discuss solutions," James said, the orange light dying out, "not share insults."

Marcus scoffed, waving his hand dismissively in the air, signaling to his guard to stand down. "Typical," he muttered.

"Excuse me?" James asked, frowning.

"Are you trying to tell me there is no bias here?" Marcus raised an eyebrow.

"This is a meeting on neutral ground, for a fair judgment of the situation," James seethed. "Believe me, if I thought the Pack was to blame, I'd be handling this very differently."

"Please, Druid, do not insult my intelligence," Marcus sighed. "There has always been a soft spot for the wolves amongst your kind."

"There has always been justice," James corrected. "And understanding."

"A debt to be returned for freeing them," Marcus spat, and from the corner of his eye James could see the muscles in Colin's body tense.

"From your shackles," James retorted. "But let's not forget that the Druids were the last line of defense against the Insurgence, when the Demons tore through your ranks and you only had us to save you."

"Yes," Marcus frowned, "you never fail to remind me."

"Because you seem to constantly forget," James hissed. "I will always have the utmost respect for you and your kind, Marcus, despite the past. We put our differences behind us long ago, when it was clear that fighting amongst ourselves opened the paths for others to tear at our throats. We've been maintaining the peace for so long, and now someone's trying to disturb that. We're here to make sure that doesn't happen."

Colin grunted. "I agree."

"Of course you do," Marcus said, sitting up straight. "Louis was murdered by a wolf. There is no denying it."

"None of the other packs would dare overstep," Colin replied, his mood still dampened by the tension in the air.

"Well, someone obviously did," Marcus spat. "We will search for whoever is responsible, and I expect the same from your family."

Marcus stood, abruptly ending the meeting without waiting for a reply. "And you, Druid," he said, turning to James. "My advice would be to tread carefully. The Druids are gone, the Hand is gone. All that remains of the past are you and that child. If someone is trying to upset the balance, I assure you that the two of you are high on their target list."

"We can handle ourselves," James assured the man.

"So could Louis," Marcus said, "and we all know how that played out. If someone was capable of killing Louis Lesoleil, then an old Druid and his niece won't be much of a challenge."

James opened his mouth to reply, then thought better of it and closed it again. He watched as the vampire led his escorts out of the Dome. James stood slowly, and turned to face his friend.

"He's right, you know," Colin said, his eyes set forward and staring at the door through which Marcus had left.

"Was it one of yours?" James asked immediately, hoping to catch the man off-guard.

Colin's eyes snapped to him, and James could see the anger reflected in them over the accusation. "Of course not."

"Another pack?"

Colin shook his head angrily. "If it was, then they'll have me to deal with." Colin stood, his towering figure shaking with contained rage. "This will not be ignored, I promise you."

James nodded. "Good. I have to bring Atlanta up to speed. She needs to be ready."

"I'll send you a pair of guards," Colin said. "Just to make sure."

James scoffed and waved away the suggestion. "Atlanta will be fine. She works better alone."

Colin gazed at his friend for a beat, then nodded and stuck out his hand. "Good luck, my friend."

James shook it then watched the Pack leave.

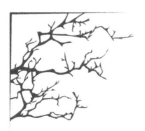

Chapter 5

"TAKE IT EASY, ATLANTA," Ryan Toller sighed. "I was just voicing my condolences. It's not such a big deal!"

They were standing behind the bleachers of Calen High's football field, Ryan in uniform and ready for practice. Atlanta stood in front of him, arms crossed over her chest.

It had taken her forever to shake off Skylar, and a bloomin' lot of effort to avoid her incessant questioning. Atlanta had spent most of the day on full alert, going through classes on cruise control while her senses were fixated on picking up any anomaly. If her uncle was right, and people were suspecting the Pack to be behind Louis' murder, then there was no telling who would come after Ryan.

It didn't help, of course, that most of her classes were shared with the heir to the Calen Pack, and that he wouldn't stop staring at her throughout the entire day. It made oblivious Skylar even more curious, which only added to the burdens of the day.

"We're trying to keep a low profile, Ryan," Atlanta scolded. "We've been doing it forever. What's the matter with you?"

Ryan frowned. "I understand playing the jock, and acting like a teenage heartthrob and all, but it doesn't mean I'm a douche."

"Well, try to be more like one!" Atlanta threw her hands in the air in exasperation. "There's an image to be kept. You know this better than any of us."

Ryan angrily pointed a finger at her. "Don't tell me what to do," he hissed. "Everybody does. Go play football, Ryan. Smile at the shallow blondes, Ryan. Date the airhead who heads the cheerleaders, Ryan."

Atlanta smiled despite herself, and it only made him angrier.

"Dammit, Atlanta, I'm sick of this!"

"Fine," Atlanta replied. "Let the energy inside you bottle up until you're shifting in the middle of cafeteria and slashing away at the other students."

A shrill whistle sounded from behind them, and Ryan looked away from Atlanta for a brief second before returning his attention to her. "Practice is starting...I gotta go." He brushed past her, shaking his head.

Atlanta grabbed him by the arm and stopped him. "We've got a few months left. Then we're home-free."

"No, we're not," Ryan said. "We're always going to be hiding in the shadows, Atlanta."

"It's for our own survival."

"Tell that to Louis," came the reply. They stared into each other's eyes for a beat before Ryan lowered his gaze. "I really am sorry about him. I kinda liked that blood-sucking idiot."

Atlanta let go of his arm and watched him trot around the side of the bleachers and back to the field. She followed him slowly, rubbing her hidden knife aimlessly as she walked up the side of the bleachers and sat down to watch the practice. Skylar would be here any minute, a ritual she forced Atlanta to share with her every Monday and Wednesday.

This time, however, Atlanta wanted to attend the Calen Wizards' practice.

Her mind went back to that fateful day when she turned twelve, when her uncle sat her down and handed her the carefully wrapped box that encased the knife she now carried. She remembered the confusion when she saw the weapon, the thought that maybe it had belonged to her parents and her uncle had decided to give it to her.

If only it had only been that. Atlanta sat down heavily on the top bleacher and ran her fingers through her hair. Her uncle's words still rang in her ears, the look on his face forever etched in her mind as he tried to explain the truth behind what was really lurking in the shadows of Calen. He had told her all about the families, the Lesoleils and the Tollers, the Fortress and the Calen Pack, the world that was hiding between the cracks and the threat of failing to maintain the balance. She remembered the tales of the Circle, the enslavement of the wolves, the role of the Druids and the Hand and, of course, the Insurgence.

She had cried for three days straight afterwards, her mind filled with monsters and nightmares, her world shattered, the reality she had come to know as absolute only a mirage. Uncle James had been patient, but after a week of self-pity and sorrow he had taken her down to the basement, the one part of the house that had always been forbidden to her, and had shown her everything.

The Skolars were the last of the Druids and, like it or not, accept it or not, this was her life. Her fate.

"Your father wouldn't have wanted this for you," her uncle had said. "The Druids have always been a brotherhood, the women fortunately left out the dangers and burdens that come with the title."

But you don't have that luxury, Atlanta thought, mouthing her uncle's words.

From then on, the basement became her home. Day and night, she trained under her uncle's relentless eye. She witnessed a completely different side to the man who had taught her how to ride a bike and had sat on the sidelines with countless mothers watching their daughters practice ballet. Through her middle school years he'd become a drill sergeant, and she'd been pushed to the very limits of her physical capabilities.

It was only when she reached high school that her Uncle James returned, the soft features and the hearty chuckles. It was also the first day he took her to the Dome and introduced her to the families. She remembered how shocked she'd been to see Ryan Toller there, the boyish look that usually plastered his face replaced by a stoic seriousness unbefitting of him. It had also been the first time she met Louis Lesoleil.

"Louis," Atlanta whispered to herself, instinctively drawing up an image of the vampire from her mind and feeling a hard stab in her chest. Smiles and shining eyes, Louis had been the closest thing to a brother she had ever known. Ever since hearing about his death she had tried to play it cool, to mask her feelings as best she could. She didn't want her uncle to worry about her, and she definitely didn't want more questions from Skylar.

Now, alone on the bleachers, she let her tears flow. Her emotions ran wild inside her, and her body shivered despite the heat. For the first time since it happened, she let Louis' death really sink in. From deep inside her she felt something burn, a new feeling she'd never experienced before, but welcomed it anyway.

It coursed through her veins like a bonfire, and within seconds threatened to overwhelm her completely. She didn't fight it, though, allowing a sharp gasp to escape her as she hunched over and began to cry.

"Atlanta!"

Atlanta's head shot up, her body suddenly stiffening with alertness at the sudden cry of her name. She looked over the field to where Ryan was waving at her and pointing. She followed his gesture, and at the far end of the field saw what he was pointing at.

There were three. Humans, she knew instantly, but from their gait and determined march towards Ryan she also knew they were being compelled. They carried their weapons menacingly, and Atlanta didn't need to wonder if the knife one of them was holding was silver or not.

She knew exactly what they were doing here.

The vampires were striking back.

Atlanta stood quickly and skipped down the bleachers, watching as two of Ryan's teammates confronted the intruders. Atlanta knew what the result of that would be, and winced when the fight broke out. She sprinted towards Ryan, her eyes flitting back and forth between him and the men. Ryan stood in his place, watching and waiting, his chest rising and falling as he breathed. She called out to him but he didn't hear her, and she silently prayed that the burst of adrenaline coursing through him didn't force him to shift.

Cries of pain sounded from the fight taking place to her right, and she resisted the urge to help. She knew that a compelled human would be next to impossible to handle, especially since they were blind to anything but their mission. It was like fighting against a brick wall that would only be stopped if knocked unconscious—or worse, killed.

And Calen High was not one of the places Atlanta wanted to be dropping bodies in.

Her eyes scanned the huddle of flying fists and grunts, a screech of pain escaping from the midst of it all. The compelled were armed, and the high school football players had little chance of holding them back without throwing some serious weight behind their fists. Her eyes met one of the intruder's, and she hesitated for a second when she saw a bright flash of red.

I've never seen that happen before.

'Red eyes' broke free from the huddle, noticed where Atlanta was running to, and immediately sprinted in her direction. He was incredibly fat, and for the briefest of moments Atlanta felt doubt creep into her. There was something different here, something off, and if she didn't figure it out in the next second or so she'd be fighting blindly against something she didn't understand.

She looked to Ryan. His eyes were turning yellow and his teeth elongating. It pushed away all her doubts and reservations. He was beginning to shift, and she needed to stop it before he transformed.

She turned sharply, changing her direction, and made straight for her attacker. The large man raced towards her with his knife held high above his head. The snarl on his face was enough to let Atlanta know that whatever thread of sanity had once been there was now gone.

She met him halfway between the huddle and Ryan. With a quick flick of her hand, she unsheathed her knife just as he brought his down in a wide arc, aiming for her neck. She blocked the blow, quickly pushing her weight against the man's arm and twisting around him. Without breaking stride she swung the handle of her own knife down hard against the base of his skull, forcing a grunt of pain from him, and quickly sheathed her weapon again.

The man crumpled in a heap at her feet, unconscious and now harmless. She jumped over him and raced towards Ryan.

"Ryan! Stop!" she hissed, and although he was watching the huddle of his teammates trying to fight the other two intruders his eyes darted for a second to look at her. "Ryan, you have to stop! Now!"

He let out a growl, a deep rumbling that seemed to echo in Atlanta's head, and she grabbed both his arms just as he was about to move to his friends' aid.

"You do this," Atlanta whispered quickly, "and you ruin everything."

"I can't stand here and do nothing," Ryan barked, his voice a deep baritone mixed with the grinding of teeth. His hazel-yellow eyes oozed fury.

"Yes, you can," Atlanta pressed, refusing to let go of his arms. "You have to."

Ryan stiffened, but stopped resisting her. "I'll have the fangs of the vampire who did this."

"We both will." She tried to calm him down more. "Right now, though, you need to ease off."

Ryan shook his head in fury and clenched his fists. Atlanta held him tight, ready to knock him down as well if he tried to do anything other than what she was ordering him to. She didn't know how the Calen Pack would react to her knocking their prince unconscious, but she hoped they might understand given the circumstances

Ryan loosened up slowly, his muscles relaxing and his fists unclenching. The yellow in his eyes faded and his fangs retracted. He sighed as his body shuddered against her grip.

"Skolar!"

Atlanta turned. The Calen Wizards coach marched up to her while nursing a nasty blow to his cheek. Behind him, the team had subdued the other two men, some taking turns at kicking them in frustration while others tried to make sure things didn't get more out of hand. One team member was being carried away, his arm bleeding profusely.

The coach stopped and looked down at the man Atlanta had knocked down, then up at her with a sly grin. "You know, it might be a good idea if you tried out for the girls' Kung Fu team," he said, moving his jaw from side to side as he winced in pain.

"Nah, Coach," one of the other team members yelled from behind him. "With skills like that, she should be on the boys' football team."

A few howled in approval, while Atlanta felt like crawling under a rock.

So much for keeping a low profile.

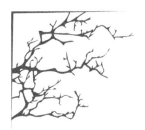

Chapter 6

AS SHE SAT ON HER BED, her earphones over her head with the music on mute, Atlanta closed her eyes and listened to her uncle downstairs. He was far from happy; the news of what had happened at Calen High had spread like wildfire through both worlds. Needless to say, her uncle was not impressed like the football players had been.

She glanced at her phone, tapped on the Whatsapp icon, and checked if Skylar had responded to her text. Still nothing. She couldn't blame her friend. Atlanta knew she wouldn't be able to keep so many secrets from her best friend for too long without something like this eventually happening. She just wished she could explain things to Skylar, rather than give her some excuse that wouldn't have made sense to a toddler let alone someone as suspicious as her best friend.

Nothing's ever easy, is it? She sighed and tossed her phone to the side, bumping her head against the wall behind her as she tried to make heads or tails out of what had happened. She'd seen a lot during her time as a Hand, but never had she come across eyes that flashed red like that. It was something entirely new, although a part of her felt there was also something vaguely familiar about it.

Where have I seen eyes like that before?

Her uncle's heavy footsteps on the stairs brought her back, and she watched the door patiently as the knob turned and her uncle stuck his head in. She forced a smile for him but he didn't return it, instead walking into her room and crossing his arms. It was a stance she'd adopted from him, but it looked far more menacing on him.

"What were you thinking?" he asked, eyeing her seriously.

Atlanta sighed and took off her headphones. "What else was I supposed to do? Ryan was going to shift, and that would've been a heck of a lot worse."

"How about running?" James asked. "It's what normal teenagers do. *Normal* female teenagers don't knock down a man with a knife and expect no one to notice."

"The team took down the other two," Atlanta argued.

"The team is a dozen football players high on testosterone looking for a fight," James snapped, clearly exasperated. "And it took all of them to take down two."

Atlanta lowered her eyes and grinned.

"It wasn't meant as a joke," James scolded. "On any other night, I would've given you a high five and a pat on the back, told you that you did a great job out there making sure the monsters stayed in the damn shadows." She looked up at him and could see the worry mixed with anger in his eyes. "This, however, was reckless. Why in the world did you take the knife with you in the first place?"

"Louis," Atlanta replied, the name enough explanation.

James lowered his arms, and shook his head as he rubbed his temple. "I understand how difficult

this is—"

"Do you?" Atlanta shot back, fighting the tears welling in her eyes.

"Yes," her uncle said, gazing at her. "I do."

"Then stop lecturing me about all this when I know you would've done the exact same thing!" Atlanta refused to back down or defend herself. "Ryan was either going to shift or be killed, most likely the former." She glared at her uncle, angry at the world and beyond confused by it. "Besides," she added lamely, "I didn't kill anyone."

James stared at her for a moment longer, and then finally nodded. "What did you see? What's got you so riled up?"

Atlanta sat up straight. "It was like they were compelled," she explained, using her hands as she talked. "At first I thought it had to be that."

"At first?"

Atlanta frowned, and tried to find a better way to explain what she'd seen. "They knew what they were doing. Except, the compelled are usually just following orders blindly. These were different...they were thinking. The one I knocked down? When he saw me, he immediately came for me. Like he knew me, or at least knew what I was, and immediately ditched Ryan for me. Compelled *never* do that."

James nodded in agreement, frowning. "Marcus assures me he's gone through the entire Fortress. This wasn't a compulsion."

"Could there be vampires outside the family?"

James shrugged. "On the other side of the ocean, maybe. But it's hard to believe Marcus wouldn't know about new vampires in our own backyard."

"There's something else." Atlanta swallowed, suddenly nervous again. "Their eyes..."

"What about them?"

"They flashed red." Atlanta shuddered, remembering it clearly. "It's almost as if they were glowing."

The older man stiffened suddenly, his mouth open and his eyes wide. His mouth closed, then opened, then closed again. Finally, he whispered, "Are you sure?"

She nodded. She'd never seen the blood rush out of her uncle's face that fast before. "Positive. Why? Do you know what they were?"

James didn't answer, his eyes shifting as he seemed to stare off into space. She could almost feel his mind working, the gears inside turning at hyper-speed as he processed the new information she had given him. The glowing eyes obviously meant something, and her uncle had the missing information that had been plaguing her for the past few hours.

"Uncle James?"

James raised his eyebrows in response, but didn't look at her.

"Uncle James!"

"Yes!" James snapped out his stupor.

"What are they?"

James licked his lips and swallowed. "Get dressed," he ordered, his face darkening as he turned to leave. "We need to get to the Dome."

"I'm already dressed."

James stopped and looked over his shoulder. "No, you're not. Get in your gear."

THE SUIT WAS DEEP CRIMSON. When worn it clung to Atlanta like a second layer of skin, but the material itself was stronger than Kevlar. The first time she laid eyes upon it, she had hated it immediately. The color, the plainness of it, and the fact that wearing it meant a needless accentuation of her curves that she was utterly uncomfortable with.

She fought long and hard against even trying it on, but her uncle had assured her that, without it, all the action she would ever see would be on TV. When she'd finally given in, she was surprised at how comfortable it really was, how much freedom of movement it allowed her and, after a multitude of training sessions with her uncle, how much protection it truly had to offer. There was also the added benefit of endless sheaths for all her weapons, including the Druid staff on her back.

Nevertheless, she made sure not to pass by any mirrors while wearing it. The fabric rose from her boots, all around her body, to where the gloves clasped on with Velcro, and finally around her neck.

"That's so the vampires don't get to you," her uncle had said with a smile.

The Druids get cloaks and hoods, she had thought, and I have to look like a freak circus stripper.

After years of donning the suit, though, she'd grown to appreciate just how important it was. She'd seen little battle outside the basement where her uncle trained her until she bled and hurt all over. Yet, the few times she had been forced to fight, the suit had definitely played a part in her survival. She could only imagine the bones that would have been broken in the places where only bruises lingered after one fight or the other.

"Ready?' James asked as she slid the last of her weapons into its respective sheath.

Atlanta nodded.

She followed her uncle into the basement, both ignoring the light switch as they made their way across the training ground. Atlanta knew every inch of the basement by heart, had been forced to train on multiple occasions with a blindfold on, and easily sidestepped the racks of weapons and punching bags that decorated the room.

With the lights on, one wouldn't imagine that a space this large could exist under the Skolar house. The ten acres of land surrounding the house had been in her family for generations, and at one point had housed a mansion that had unfortunately been burned down during the Insurgence. All that remained were the passageways under the surface that branched out to various parts of the city. Of course, Calen had almost doubled in size in the past thirty years alone, but without the full force of the Druids the tunnels never caught up.

Still, Atlanta was satisfied with the current expansiveness of the network. The passages still led to the most important parts of the city, and from there it was never far to where she wanted to be. Besides, it wasn't like she was wearing her crimson suit all the time. Her uncle's sedan was still more than enough to get her where she wanted to go on regular nights.

She followed her uncle to the far side of the basement, where he pushed his hand against a loose stone in the wall. A loud click echoed, and the makeshift shelf of books slid open on its hinges and opened into a staircase that descended into the tunnels below. They made their way down, and as they entered a small vestibule fluorescent lights flickered on. Two Ducatis stood side by side in the center of the vestibule, waiting for their riders.

"Are you going to tell me what's gotten you so worked up?" Atlanta asked, looking over at her uncle as he slid his own staff across his back and tossed her helmet to her.

"Nothing," he muttered.

Atlanta paused, raising an eyebrow at him as he tightened his cloak around his own suit, a black replica of her own. "I thought we were past keeping secrets from each other."

"Believe me," her uncle replied with a weak smile, "there are some secrets you'll wish you never knew."

"You aren't helping."

"Just get on your bike," James gestured. "The sooner we get to the Dome, the sooner I can put my worries at ease."

Atlanta pulled her helmet on and straddled her bike, turning the key and letting the engine roar. "What's at the Dome anyway?" she asked, trying to remember anything out of the ordinary she might have overlooked on her previous visits.

"A door," James replied.

"A door?"

"Yeah," came the short reply as her uncle pulled on his own helmet. "I just want to make sure it's still locked."

She frowned in confusion as her uncle gunned his own engine, motioned to her, and sped down the passageway. From somewhere deep inside her a tingling formed, and began to slowly spread through her body. She shook it away, revved the engine, and followed her uncle into the darkness.

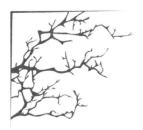

Chapter 7

THE DARKNESS SLOWLY decomposed into flickers of neon lights that raced to brighten the way to their charging Ducatis. Confusion ran through her veins like a river that coursed through indefinite paths. She firmly grabbed the handles of her rumbling bike, tightening to try to compose her heart's endless throbbing.

Atlanta knew James was focused, his gaze fixed into the distance, the sound of his bike's engine roaring and vibrating over the rain-stained streets of the city. The redness of the walls around the ancient door continued to flicker around every street lamp. The route to the Dome had never felt longer. Atlanta left the navigation to the automation of her mind while the rest of her thoughts rolled on like a thunderstorm, echoing the fear of an unexpected source of malice. She thought of the Insurgence over and over, trying to figure out what it meant and what had her uncle so uneasy. Riding felt as if they were in a scene from one of her nightmares from recent nights.

Those red, glaring eyes. The image popped into her mind; she couldn't erase it.

All her years as a Druid couldn't supply her with the proper imagination to fantasize of the oncoming dread she felt quivering through the exhaust of her uncle's speeding bike. All she could do was hope that whatever door James was talking about would be just a fragment of the instability Louis' murder had caused.

The roar of the engines began to calm as the dry fountains around the Dome made their appearance. The forests behind the Dome disappeared as the mist soared high, like the smoke of a burning empire. The structure exhaled myriad legacies and stories that were carved into the smoky, grey stone walls. On top of the structure was a huge marble dome. The most mesmerizing aspect of the dome was that it was half red conglomerate, and the other half was adorned with bedazzling dark blue marble.

The stone sculptures of the monsters and gargoyles seemed to glare at Atlanta as she staggered off her bike. She glared at the sculptures, trying to calm herself with the thought that evil being frozen and cemented in these forms was a way to contain it.

"Atlanta, they won't attack you!" James snapped as he bolted to the brown door of the Dome.

She shook her head and buried the paralyzing fear beneath a false sense of security, and tried to compose herself. "Sorry, I just..." she mumbled. "Never mind." She sighed the words and hurried behind James, looking back once more before the shadows of the entrance met the moonlight and the statues disappeared from view.

Inside, there was vast emptiness that encompassed the place, dark grey walls that stood heavy with no ornaments, only frames of paintings that were single colored. Each seemed to be a shade of blue or red.

A stairway leading up to the table where the families met seemed to be the only structure that was built-in. The side of the stairway was plated with gold, which shone through the blackened corners of the Dome.

"We've got to move quickly," James snapped out in a quiet, worried voice.

Atlanta nodded, not sure if he was talking to himself or her.

Their footsteps echoed as James led the way towards the stairway. Atlanta looked up and could see the area where the stone table was set. She could feel Louis' presence in every corner of the place, could hear his arrogant laughter. Most terrifying, though: she swore she could almost hear his panting as he ran, trying to escape his inevitable death.

"Not up," James said as he slowly moved his hand on the surface of the wall at the bottom of the staircase.

"Since when has there been any other way to the table?" she asked in confusion.

"Wait for it..." He continued moving along the wall. "See the painting with the darkest shade of blue?"

"I could barely tell the color of your suit in here." She shook her head, trying to focus better in the darkness.

"First painting on the corner, right there," he said, pointing at an almost-crooked painting right across from where the staircase was. "At its top right edge there's a small sphere. Pull the sphere, and a long needle will stretch out. Get it," he whispered to her as he smeared the dust on parts of the wall with his fingers, drawing small circles into the surface.

Atlanta sprinted to the painting. The grey frame was camouflaged with the wall. She slid her hand behind the top edge and cautiously moved her fingers around until something pricked the tip of her finger. Using her finger and thumb, she lifted the thin pin out. The silver needle glittered in the dark as she ran back to James and gave it to him.

He'd been drawing, or something, in the years of collected dust the entire time. The complete swirl intertwined with similar curves of the wall's clean grey. One of his fingers pressed beside a small, almost unnoticeable, hole in the wall.

She glanced around in confusion, trying to read through the emptiness that engulfed every corner of the Dome. Her eyes darted from corner to corner and back to where James seemed to still be frantically drawing. "Are you going to tell me what all this is about now?" she asked, almost hesitatingly.

"There'll be time for stories later," James replied in a monotone. "Just slowly slide it in there," he muttered, apparently to himself. "Rotate this here, and...there we go."

Just as his words subsided, a strident vibration of the friction of the wall resounded through every corner of the Dome. The dust on the walls sprang up in clouds of smoky grey. The wall began to slide behind itself, revealing a passage to a room right under the stone table above.

The Dome, as its outside blue and red colors showed, was a symbol of peace and unity between two families that, for centuries, were embroiled in conflict. Its center was the meeting room where conflicts were resolved and discussions dissolved into solutions.

Atlanta sucked in a sharp breath. The peace that held everything together was a joke. She realized it now. Just a cloth to the eyes. Underneath was a deep, dark, untold secret. Hidden so the peace would remain undisturbed.

"Stay at the door," James ordered as he walked slowly into the passage. "No one comes in until I get out. Got it?"

"Yeah." She stared into the darkness, terror rushing through her veins. "Is the door in there? What if it's open?"

"That's what I'm going to find out. No one follows me down there, and if I don't come back pull the needle from the wall and find Marcus." He didn't wait for her to reply, his voice sinking into the shadows that engulfed room behind the hidden door.

A protest on her lips, she pressed them tight to stop the words from escaping. She hated not knowing what to expect, plus she was furious with her uncle for thinking he was protecting her by keeping secrets. But most of all, she felt her chest sending shivers down to her feet. Her mind shouted at her to run, not to fight, not to stand and protect the door. She hugged herself. The fear of facing what took away Louis, the fear of it reaching James before it found her, raced through her mind.

Why are you so afraid? she asked herself.

Was it the fear of the unknown, the fear of the unfamiliar? Or an evil so unexplainable she didn't have the tools to defeat it?

Just as that thought echoed in her head a deep growl resounded through the Dome, shaking the very core of her being. It wasn't an unfamiliar sound. It was something she had heard that morning. Not the howling of the winds outside, it was closer. And terrifying.

She spun around when she remembered what the sound signaled.

She stared blindly and, for a moment, forgot where she was. She forgot about her uncle in the room below. She forgot about the sculptures outside the Dome, about the shuddering growl that shook the Dome a second ago. Instead, she wished she could forget the existence of the moment she was in now.

The silence lasted only a second. And it wasn't because of the absence of sound, but because her thoughts fell to a comatose state at the person in front of her.

When her eyes met with Ryan Toller's.

His were blazing red.

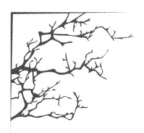

Chapter 8

A CENTURY AGO...

The sea was bloody red and the skies a dirty grey. The winds howled as the thunder roared out its warning. The city of Calen stood desolate against the wars going on inside it. Red was the color that could be seen radiating through its morning sky. The Vamps were at the height of their cannibalistic nature, their diet of human blood served warm in the morning heat or cold in the dead of the night.

In the forests surrounding the city, magic spiraled around every bush and tree. At night, the witches spread through the forests surrounding the city, their words echoing among the evergreens. A velvet ring radiated and encircled the city, preventing anyone from leaving; not because the witches were ruling, but rather in fear of the wrath of the Vamps.

With every passing night, when the moon hung proud and white, the number of witches grew smaller and smaller. More fell to the pinch of teeth, their green blood coursing through vampire's veins. The stronger the Vamps grew, the more their reign over Calen persisted.

"Perceive us, for when all be gone we remain," rang a voice so mellow, the trees sighed and breathed in reply. "All that is now is for all that's to come, a light for you and me," she sang, humming tunes that pulled the ravens down from the skies, to the curves of her shoulders.

He watched her in the shadows, anger pouring from him and running off his skin in cold waves.

She had deep green eyes; her hair hung down to her knees in shades of black and grey. Her lips were two crescent moons embracing at the bottom of her face. "Marcus, Marcus, Marcus," she said, breaking into another round of ironic yet assured laughter. "I see the girls' spells couldn't stop you from coming here."

"You overestimate your children, Adelaide," Marcus replied, his voice deep.

"I see your centuries of loneliness are finally taking a toll on you. You cannot spend a day without seeing your dear Adelaide," she said, then broke again into a laughter so loud birds flew to hide behind the moon. All but the ravens; they stayed on her shoulders and glared with flaming red eyes into Marcus' self-assured, proud stance.

"Have you gone madder than you already are?" hissed Marcus, his rage circling the heaviness of his fangs.

"Mad!" she exclaimed sarcastically. "Madness is my sanity as long as your kind is setting the rules. You're misguided, my dear. Keeping the pack underground is no pledge to the dominance of your kind, and neither will all the witches' blood feed you with the power to do anything but sigh to the moon when the force arrives."

Adelaide strode through the brush as she lay words just like she cast spells. She waved her hands, grazing every tree which broke into laughter at her soft touch. Her back was turned to Marcus as she began to join in with the laughter of the trees.

Her laughter was brought to an abrupt halt as Marcus's breath howled around the veins on her neck, his hands grasping her wrists, clotting the green in her blood.

But Adelaide didn't even sigh. Her cheeks stretched and her teeth shone in the dead of the forest night. The ravens were holding their wings just above Marcus' broad back.

"How dare you mock my kind with your witchery," he hissed, his voice echoing past the stiffness of his fangs. "Cementing Philip is the last of your countless atrocities. Your sorcery has passed the line of my leniency."

Adelaide's laughter grew darker and louder, her arms slowly sliding out of Marcus's firm grip. With the lightest of movement, she broke free from the pressure of his clenching body. Marcus was frozen still, and she moved away from him as if he were a chair.

He glared at her, his movements now solidified. Only his eyes gave way, rolling around and radiating his immense rage.

"You couldn't wait until I offered my help. Patience, my dear, patience," scoffed Adelaide. "You enlighten me with your fierceness, beast. And a beautiful animal you are." She roared out more of her mocking laughter.

She walked around his half-bent, fixed, and frozen body, her swirling arms grabbing the back of his head. She pulled out a strand of his dark hair. She came closer to the contracted, stiff muscles of his face, her green eyes an infinite tunnel meeting with his bloodshot ones. "The blood of a Vamp is all I needed," she whispered, "but Philip was a weak bloodsucker. However, you, my dear, have centuries of life coursing through your black veins. You are one of them, the Firsts." She smiled at him, and the way her lips curled made her look even more menacing. "Haven't you heard, my dear Marcus, that the Druids are coming to Calen? They'll be there and you'll be here for a night and, even better, a day. You'll gaze upon your loving sun."

Adelaide's hands suddenly glowed green, creeping down Marcus' skin. Her fingers slid down on his throbbing chest and the green glow rested on his heart. She pushed her hands, penetrating the chambers of his heart, and her fingers caressed the arteries inside his chest. She pulled out her hands, softly, as the blood gushed up towards his head. Marcus' head turned a darker shade of red, his fangs dripping violet blood.

His eyes jerked side to side as he tried to break free.

A wine glass appeared in Adelaide's hands. She filled it with his blood. "I'll leave you to your thoughts now, my dear. I have hybrids I need to bear. It was enchanting to see you." She rolled out her last strain of laughter. Her crescent lips laid a soft kiss on Marcus' upper lip, which silently quivered with his suppressed rage.

"Oh dear, have I forgotten to return your beloved voice? There you go," she whispered as her feet soared and her body glowed with the witches' evergreen.

Marcus roared out a growl that echoed through the forest and resounded in the ear of every Vamp in Calen. But it wasn't the time for the Vamps to come save their master, for at that time the Druids were at the gates of Calen.

SHE EYED THE SKIES as their velvety purple smoothness was witness to the birth of a power that would soon shake Calen. An empire of embers descended, and fell around her as the ravens flew against the sighing winds. On the hilltop where the grass whispered words, and stars could be seen frowning, her deep green eyes stood watch over Calen as it burned. The vampires were wailing, the wolves running free, and the Druids were sweeping every corner of the city, their air vaporizing every shackle and setting free the once-damned beasts of Calen.

But the power that was being born wasn't the power of the Druids, for that had existed decades before this time. In that moment, something far more expressionless was being brought to life.

For years, Adelaide had been the mother of all witches, the atom of sorcery, the enchantress. Her history in Calen was not recognized by many, and not because her power was benign in the city but rather because she made sure her presence was to be concealed, and her power undermined. Adelaide didn't want to be acknowledged, because acknowledgement meant the possibility of defiance. Her lust for power was deeper than a vampire's lust for blood, much more intense than a wolf's hunger and longing for a full moon. She never needed to wear a cloak of sanity and wander the streets, casting spells and enchanting the inhabitants of the city, for from the hilltop where her oak tree stood watch over Calen, her thoughts and desires prowled the night and ensured her rule over the city.

Marcus was the first to notice the peculiarity in the nights when green mist would encompass the city sky. In his many centuries of life, he had crossed paths with witches in many of the cities he had wandered. But none of them ever dared to move an inch. They all lurked in the shadows of the forests, petting snakes and turning doves and eagles into ravens. To the Vamps they were never an enemy: they were prey. Their green blood when drank by a vampire would enhance his or her powers for days, maybe months, giving them a surge of unparalleled speed and strength.

Once, some witches were found in the basements of the city. Marcus butchered them with no hesitation, their blood seeping into his veins, giving him and his kind the power they needed to capture all the werewolves and shackle them.

Now the Druids had come to Calen, freeing the werewolves, and the reign of the Vamps was coming to an end. They were no longer an unprecedented power. The Druids preached coexistence, where every race was equal. The unwise vampires were slayed, and the ones high on witches' blood were brought to their knees, flailing. They were facing both the slayers and the werewolves, and the city was in flames.

Adelaide sighed. She watched as the window of opportunity was pierced with gleams of supremacy. She was not witnessing a scene that was alien to her deep green eyes; she had, after all, foreseen the fall of the lustful Vamps.

Shadows circled her. The mouthful of conjurations made the grass flicker in obedience. Her eyes gleamed hungry for the moments yet to come. Marcus' blood was carried by the winds that bowed to her enchanting words, circling around the shadows.

"It is time and only time that will whisper this unveiling." She laid the words down in melodies.

The purple skies thundered on and a dark grey cloud descended on the hilltop, right above the winds that carried the vampire's blood. Adelaide pierced her arm with her claw-like nails, and her green blood came rushing out rhythmically to the turning of the winds. Her blood danced around and flew to the darkened clouds. She laid her runes in symphonies that hypnotized the cloud bearing the blood. Inside it, the vampire's blood orbited the witch's until, in moments, the rings of droplets were like two perfect circles entwined, a darker shade of green, and a greener shade of red.

The silhouettes paraded and danced. They laughed in excitement and in reckoning of their becoming. They were more spirits than just shadows; under the magic of Adelaide, the mere unmoved became an emblem of that which laughed and giggled.

The bloody rain drizzled on the shadows and their naked skin was unveiled by the green mist that orbited them. Their form tangible, the silhouettes had become an itching and the itching a thought. The thought became a multitude of itself and the myriad became desires. The desires all intertwined, magnified, and their forced direction was Adelaide's pounding heart. And hence the malice was instilled in their fresh minds before the sun could have a chance to shine.

"To each one their name, my lovely children," she whispered to them between breaking breaths as her laughter roared on. "Wandering in the forests isn't your fate like mine had been. You will live in the flames of this city behind you. It's yours!"

She felt like a demigod as her words sprang out along with the fore-seeing of Calen as a ring on her green, glowing fingers.

"Your orders, Mother," the newly birthed echoed in one thundering voice, mixed with the croaks of the ravens and the laughter of the trees.

Adelaide laughed, almost shaking the core of the city with the malevolence that gushed through her voice. "Bring me Calen," she sang in between her laughs as silence broke on the hilltop. "Set the gargoyles free, and unleash all the beasts in statues and carvings. Let all the trapped spirits free."

The wind picked up and swirled viciously.

"Bring me Calen!" she screamed as the darkened green mist flew from her crescent lips.

There was more than a dozen of them. Their fangs stretched out from their jaws, their figures lined with slightly visible green silhouettes, their movements in rhythm with Adelaide's beating heart. They were more powerful than anything the city had ever seen, a hybrid, a vampire's speed and strength oozing out from their breaths, and magic carved into their every bone.

And the flames in Calen singed on.

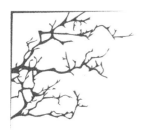

Chapter 9

The moonlight was a symphony that laid its white rays in tune with the greenery of the forest behind the Dome. Ravens descended 'round the marble stone, echoing their croaks in cryptic wonder. A deep howling trembled all that was still around the Dome, and the sound of the heavy pounding of Atlanta's heart rode the whispers of the wind and paraded through the atmosphere of Calen.

She swallowed. Her mouth had gone dry and she absently tried to wet it again. She couldn't take her eyes off Ryan.

His jaw protruded, the sharpness of his teeth flashing again the moonlight shining into the Dome. His growl repeatedly quivered the crevices of the structure and reverberated against the walls. The grey and white fur extending from his arms, back, and head bent as if the earth were pulling his upper body towards the floor. His eyes were surrounded by his glittering fur and were glowing a dull red.

Atlanta stood frozen. She'd seen Ryan turn before, but whenever he had his eyes were glaring at an enemy, a threat. This time they were fixated on her, and he was approaching with the swiftness of a predator. It wasn't a secret; with all her strength, she felt like nothing but prey. Or maybe it was her heart climbing out of her chest, taking peeks to reassure her that it was all a dream and she should remain still, unmoved.

"Ryan!" she cried out in an effort to reach him, to knock some sense into him.

He paused momentarily in his advance, his only response a deeper growl echoing from inside his chest, his red eyes narrowing in on her.

He took a stealthy step forward, his shoulders dropping as he took another advancing step.

"Ryan!" she tried again. "What's gotten into you?" She watched his every move, anticipating the attack at any moment. He was coming for her. She squatted, trying to prepare for his launch and hoping she could stop him without killing him. She had nothing to fight with and this was her friend. She didn't want to kill him. Except, his advance warned her he thought completely differently.

Out the darkness behind her, James bolted out the secret door. His frantic movement turned Ryan's focus to him.

James' head jerked into the direction of the red glow shining his way. He shoved Atlanta out of the way and stood to face Ryan. Before the adrenaline had the chance to rush through his body, the wolf surged at him. In the next instant, James was flying through the air. His body hovered a second, silhouetted by the Dome's night sky colors shining through the glass. Then his back hammered against one of the grey stone walls.

He didn't move from his crumpled heap.

Atlanta broke from her shock and slid her knife from the back of her suit. A sudden wind outside sounded like it was being pierced by a force so large, it cried out in warning. The door of the Dome slammed open and the classical air of power followed in, orbiting a dark, caped figure's frame.

Marcus. Where had he come from?

"The werewolves aren't stopping at Louis, I see," he growled as he broke in. Every stone in the Dome magnified his presence.

Ryan turned away from Atlanta. His eyes fired towards Marcus, and before the vampire could blink the wolf leapt towards him. Ryan slammed into Marcus, crushing his body into the stone floor.

Marcus roared in anger, pinned down by the beast's unparalleled force. His eyes met the blazing redness in Ryan's.

Atlanta watched, unsure of what to do. Step in and help? But who was she supposed to help?

A gasp from Marcus caught her attention.

"Druid," he said in an odd tone. "The pack isn't the enemy. The wolves didn't kill Louis."

"What?" whispered Atlanta.

"These red eyes did." Marcus brought his arms up and held the wolf at bay. "A long time ago, someone attacked me. A witch." He struggled as Ryan's teeth bit at the air between them, trying to tear skin. Marcus held him back, talking to Atlanta, or himself, she wasn't quite sure. "Adelaide. The green eyes, the green blood, the..." His head jerked to the side as he avoided Ryan's gnashing jaw. "She froze my body in the forest and stole... ripped my blood from me. My very essence stolen. She left me powerless—for a while." Marcus curled his hands into fists, grabbing fur in chunks. He roared as he threw Ryan off him.

Atlanta watched, paralyzed, glimpsing her uncle's fallen body. Had he heard Marcus right? Was her uncle even alive? Another crash had her jumping out of the way. This wasn't the kind of fight that would end well. One of them was going to die. Any death would cause an endless surge of blood, and the current throbbing of her heart would only be a metaphor of the chaos she would yet have to face.

Their howls echoed in the night, the fight an endless bombarding of two opposites. There was nothing Atlanta could do but try to protect her uncle from swinging fists, stomping legs, and sharp teeth.

The wolf let out a growl before launching again at Marcus. The vampire shifted his body away as Ryan missed him by an inch. His fur was pulled from his back as Marcus' claws dug into him. Marcus lifted Ryan up with one arm and slammed him onto the floor beneath his feet, another carving on the floor—this time a wolf entwined with the vampire's body.

Marcus thrust his arm through the air, thundering into the wolf's jaw. Bones cracked as dark blue blood coursed out of Ryan's body.

Marcus was clearly enraged, his power unparalleled. No defiance could shake his determination to break the wolf and kill it. Probably scattering the ashes across every darkened corner of the Dome. He marched toward the fallen body of the wolf and wrapped his hands around the back of his head, his claws digging into Ryan's neck.

He clearly wasn't afraid of being bitten by the wolf. He wasn't going to hesitate putting his hand into its mouth and pulling out Ryan's heart.

Atlanta sank to her knees at the sight of Ryan. She couldn't believe it. Louis, and now Ryan. Her perception only felt her heart slowing down to less than a beat per second, trying to escape the moment. Myriad feelings surged through her veins; flashes of Ryan walking down the corridors of Calen High played in her mind. She was losing someone who made her heart skip a beat in his presence.

Suddenly she was grabbed from behind and carried towards the frightening scene as Marcus was about to end Ryan's life. She flew through the air, crashing toward the two creatures, unable to stop and clueless as to what was happening.

There was an abrupt flash of green light, followed by a horrific growl, and then dead silence.

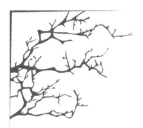

Chapter 10

THE BLUR WAS SHARPENING, the vagueness filtering between her eyelashes unfolding as the fluorescent lights flickered. Her suit sparkled under the beams of light that encompassed the basement of her house. As her brain slowly processed the colors of the room the picture became clearer, and James' figure appeared across from her.

The basement's white brick walls encompassed the vast space. Two bookshelves met in the corner. On the other side of the stairway was an area of the basement that Atlanta barely even noticed. It was at most times dark, and all that could be seen was a long wooden table with casters on its legs and sheets on top of it.

Atlanta was on the couch by the bookshelves.

My head, she thought. *What happened?*

She glanced at the other side of the basement where James was standing by the table. The last thing she remembered was her uncle lying on the floor of the Dome, unconscious and badly hurt. Slowly, the scene rushed back to her in waves: the howl of the wolf, Ryan's enflamed red eyes, and the brawl with Marcus. The memory that seemed rushed, packed into a moment like a scene badly written, was the green glow that surrounded her as she was carried towards Marcus and Ryan in what seemed to be the fatal moment of their conflict. It seemed almost like a subconscious memory, a broken fragment of a dream.

How did we get back here?

Atlanta stood up. Her feet staggered as her suit stiffened her muscles and acted like a pillar to her legs. She squinted into the darkness. James' fingers were glowing green, and on the table in front of him lay Ryan Toller, unconscious and bruised.

She felt something drop into the pit of her stomach. *Ryan!*

"Uncle James?" Her voice came in a whisper that stuttered as worry glazed the tip of her tongue. "How is he?"

"I took care of the broken bones," James sighed. "It was pretty bad. Marcus took centuries of rage out on him."

Atlanta frowned as she moved closer to the table. Her uncle touched her arm briefly, an attempt to comfort her, but she hardly noticed. All she could think about was Ryan.

"I remember he was going to attack me," she said, gazing at Ryan's closed lids. "Something wasn't right, and the eyes, they were glowing red, like the ones I saw earlier." She was rambling, almost in despair, her mind grasping for an answer to what she had just witnessed.

Ryan lay completely still, his chest rising and falling slowly, weakly. James had brought him close to revitalization. His thick black hair fell back like a pillow to his head. His body was covered in the green sheets that were almost always in the basement. Atlanta gazed at his face, her emotions rushing back and forth, from fear to confusion to a restless need to know the depth of what had happened. She needed to be assured, and she needed to understand.

"The door was closed," James said, his voice soft, "and Ryan will heal fully in a couple of days. The rest of his wounds need to be taken care of."

"And the red eyes?" she asked in frustration, her voice seeping through the tiny gaps between her gritted teeth, her eyes glowing with the surge of tears rushing to take over her now-fading composure. *Why won't he give me a straight answer?*

"He was compelled," her uncle replied dismissively, obviously not planning to say more. He was walking to the other side of the basement. The bookshelf screeched on its hinges and the secret passage opened as he hurried inside.

NEVER LOOK BACK 57

"Take care of Ryan till I get back." He turned and gave her a weary smile. "And don't worry. He won't bite." The bookshelf closed behind him.

"Compelled?" she muttered to herself. *How can a Werewolf be compelled?* She thought her uncle had finally given her an answer to what was happening, but it only confused her more. Vampires were the ones capable of compelling, but they couldn't compel a Werewolf. That defied the balance of nature. And she couldn't remember ever seeing a compelled person—or thing—having red eyes.

Her body suddenly convulsed at the thought of Marcus being at the root of all this. It explained why he'd come rushing to the Dome.

But he wouldn't kill a Vamp.

He'd never kill Louis.

A painful groan brought her attention back to the present and she focused, letting her eyes adjust to the dimness of the room.

Ryan's dark green eyes fluttered and another groan escaped his lips. The movement of his head broke his breathing as he came to. His arms and legs were tied to the table with silver binders. James had made sure the boy's movements were restricted until he came back.

"At-lanta?" Ryan's voice broke. He tried to get up, but the tension in the binders smacked him back onto the table. He let out a half-growl/half-groan as his spine echoed the strain of the cracked bones.

"Easy there," she whispered, coming closer to him, hesitating before she slid her fingers through his. "Don't try to move, Ryan. Let me take care of those wounds first."

Ryan started at her with slightly unfocused, wide eyes. It was clear he had no idea where he was or why he was in so much pain. "What happened?" he asked, grimacing, his eyes closing for a moment. "Last I remember I told Colin about what happened in the field, and I went up to my room..." His voice flattened at the last words. Atlanta could see the confusion in his eyes, his attempt to make sense of where he was and what was happening.

"James said you were compelled," Atlanta explained. "That's probably why you can't remember."

"Compelled?" he hissed, and then scoffed. Or at least tried to. It came out more like a painful cough. "That's ridiculous!" He tried to get up again and slammed back down. He groaned as the muscles in his wrist tightened and his hand gripped Atlanta's more firmly.

"Easy, Ryan; you're hurt."

"What the...What happened?" he repeated, his voice sinking in the twitching of his body and the pain in his shoulders.

"I told Uncle James about what happened in the field." She kept her voice low, trying to soothe his discomfort. "The red eyes. It makes sense now that they were compelled. But when I told Uncle James about it, he didn't react the way I thought he would. It was as if his thoughts froze or something. He didn't explain anything. I can bet, though, that he knows what they meant." Her expression was burdened. "We set out for the Dome; he said something about a door and checking to make sure it was closed." She paused, not sure how to explain what happened next.

"And?" he pressed her.

"When we got there...you were there."

"I don't remember going to the Dome." He shook his head. "The last thing I remember, I was in my room." His deep green eyes were suddenly shadowed by his dilating pupils, and he looked as if he was having an epiphany, a deep reckoning of some sort. "I remember something," he said suddenly. "Birds! Huge, black ones. At my window!

"*Birds*?"

"Their eyes were glowing red. Crows, I think."

Atlanta crossed her arms and glared at her friend. This was serious and he wanted to joke around? "Not funny. At all."

"I'm serious. I remember seeing them. Ravens, not crows.," he said, although a little hesitantly, as if his mind was playing tricks on him. "I swear I saw them." He chewed his lower lip. "It wasn't a dream, right?

No. I'm pretty sure they were there. Pecking on my window...or something." The last part sounded as if he was talking to himself.

Atlanta sighed. He'd hit his head pretty hard. Possibly had a concussion. "Don't worry. It's all right. Look, I'm going to get the bandages from upstairs—"

"Wait," he whispered, tightening his grip on her hand as she turned to go. His hold sent shivers through her body. He looked down at her hand from the corner of his eye, and with a sigh said, "Thank you."

She smiled briefly and their eyes fixed onto each another. "It's okay." She turned around and made her way upstairs. She felt her cheeks heat and the burn creep down her neck.

Was she blushing? Really? "Ravens," she chuckled, trying to change where her mind was going. She walked into the hallway, her heart easing and lightening with every step. She was smiling, and it annoyed her that she was. She wasn't much drawn towards the feeling, but apparently the feeling was drawing her near. She felt a weird warmth take over her body, the back of her neck tingling as the beating of her heart steadily found a certain comforting consistency.

She turned on the lights and made her way to the kitchen. The maroon walls could camouflage the redness of her cheeks. She almost forgot where the bandages were. Her thoughts were an array of metaphors and lines that tore and strained to rhyme.

A wind rustled her hair, and when she looked to the side something peculiar stood at the doorstep.

What the—? Atlanta froze, staring at the dark silhouette. His broad shoulders were filling the entrance. The door was open but he was standing behind it, almost in politeness, hesitant to enter. His cloak in rhythm with the night's winds and his shadow stretching far behind him, he lifted his head and a part of his dark brown hair flickered from under his hood. His eyes were immersed in the shadows.

Who... Her thought never finished as something banged against the window, and she turned to see what was there.

A black bird, probably a raven, fluttered just outside, its eyes glowing red. It cawed and then flapped its wings before flying away.

The figure at the door remained.

Ice-cold fear race through her, and almost instinctively she reached for her weapon. Her hand closed on air. *They're freakin' downstairs,* she cursed, suddenly feeling very naked without her usual array of protective gear.

The silhouette shook, and she braced herself for an attack.

But it didn't come.

Atlanta stood completely still. She shook her head and then she crouched, ready to protect herself, then blinked in surprise.

The figure was gone.

The door stood open and she hurried towards it, searching for the shadow everywhere, her eyes scanning the darkness around the house. When she found nothing, she shut the door and stood with her back against it.

What was that? She could feel her heart hammering in her chest, threatening to jump out at any moment. She tried to control her breathing, and after a few minutes finally found the strength to push away from the door and move back to the kitchen. Her mind was playing tricks on her.

She rubbed her hands, trying to warm them. The chill that raced through her, though, never left.

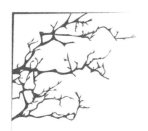

Chapter 11

THE NIGHT PASSED AS the voices in Atlanta's head settled like dust falling from the wind. The figure that she thought she'd seen by the door slowly withdrew to the recesses of her mind and settled on being a figment of her imagination.

Yet the raven flickered at the forefront. She was too scared to say that she'd seen it out loud, though. She'd scoffed at Ryan when he'd mentioned it.

She double-checked that the door was locked and headed downstairs to Ryan. They talked for hours as the hands of time slowly made moved forward. She told him the grim details of what had happened at the Dome. How his subconscious beast took over, his red eyes glaring at her, and how he was a moment away from attacking her. Ryan's body twitched as denial surged through him. He argued it hadn't happened—it couldn't have happened. And yet the bruises and chains on his body proved otherwise. They couldn't understand how he could have been compelled, but as they continued to discuss it seemed more likely that it wasn't a vampire who'd done the compelling.

But what?

None of it made sense.

Wolves couldn't be compelled. Right?

Their ideas and assumptions began to dissolve when James came back later that night, his features twisted, oozing weariness and a certain air of anxious frustration. He sat down on the beige couch in the basement and sighed.

Atlanta watched her uncle carefully, fighting the urge to burst out and demand answers. "Uncle James?"

James gazed up at her with tired eyes, the look there a mix of sympathy and fatherly protection. It was clear that he was wrestling with something. Her uncle had spent her entire life protecting her, arming her with what she needed to survive in the shadows of Calen's underworld, but always careful to keep her out of harm's way. It was written all over his face, the conflict between giving her what she needed and trying to shield her from it at the same time.

Not anymore, Atlanta thought, and she held his gaze. He needed to understand that she wouldn't let up. It was time she knew it all.

James coughed, ran a hand through his hair, and took a deep breath. "It was a little over a century ago," James started, looking at both his listeners. "Calen was mostly ruled by the vampires at the time, Marcus their leader. The werewolves were in shackles and locked away. It was unheard of, nature usually finding a balance so that neither of the two could truly hold power over the other. But the Vamps found a way to upset that balance. They discovered a way to enhance their powers, a way to give them the jump they needed to get rid of the werewolves."

"How did they do that?" Ryan demanded.

James gazed at him for a moment, and Atlanta could see the sadness in her uncle's eyes. "Drinking witch's blood," he finally replied.

Atlanta met her uncle's gaze. *Witches?*

"The witches in Calen were mediocre in strength. They never sought any power. They existed among the people, hidden, and their sorcery went mostly unnoticed for years. The vampires' lust for power drove the witches out to the forests around Calen, and it was there that they dwindled in number; yet their power increased. Adelaide was the mother witch, the enchantress, the most powerful of all witches. She'd been alive for centuries. Her ability to change her form made her invisible to the predators, and her great powers were obscured. In her possession for centuries was what the witches called 'The Charm to Oblivion,' a book that had the spells and runes written by witches from ancient times, passed down to the mother witch every millennium. Its sacredness bestowed upon her the ability to stay alive until time moved from one millennium to the other. She couldn't be killed." James's voice settled down as he took a moment to sigh. His eyes rolled over to the top right corner of the room as he began contemplating the remainder of the story.

"What happened?" Atlanta whispered, needing to know yet terrified to hear the rest.

James fixed his sight on Atlanta and began again. "Your great-grandfather, my grandfather," he told her, "was leading the forces of the Druids into Calen. They came in knowing that the greatest surge of supernatural existed in this city. Also, Colin's grandfather was an old friend of your great-grandfather, and he sent for help from the Druids. The Druids came to Calen with only one goal: the freedom of the werewolves. By then the vampires were weaker than before. It seemed...peculiar. Marcus had disappeared, and without their leader they were scattered."

"Serves 'em right," Ryan muttered, and clamped his mouth shut when Atlanta shot him a warning look.

"Some still fought," James continued, "but were mostly overpowered by the combined Druid and Werewolf forces. The Druids were experienced in slaying vampires. They knew their weaknesses, and their blades ran through them as one Druid would take on three vampires at a time. They knew nothing of what was hiding in the forests. They couldn't possibly foresee the malice that the enchantress Adelaide had prepared. The fires in Calen towered high above the clouds when the green mist came. It fell from the forests and engulfed the city. The common people stayed in their homes, locked themselves in their basements, and dwelled in fear of the carnage that was eating the streets." He sighed, as if looking back at the carnage through his own eyes. "No one expected what happened next. How could they? Everyone knew who their enemy was, whether vampire, Werewolf, or Druid. But when the mist came, something dark broke free." James stopped, his head sinking.

He looks tired, Atlanta thought to herself, and a part of her wanted to tell him to stop; that it was okay. He didn't need to continue. The recollection seemed to be taking a peculiar toll on him. Still, she needed to know. *If we're going to face whatever's out there, he needs to tell me everything.* "What happened?"

"The land where the Dome now exists had been a palace with towering, ten-yard walls surrounding it. Some of the Druids and Werewolves had been cornered by the Vamps in the palace. Then the strangest thing happened. Through the ancient windows of the palace, those inside witnessed black, tar-like liquid falling from the skies. It fell upon the vampires around the walls, dissipating them completely. Their ashes remained on the bricks of the walls and their fangs became nothing but dust in the wind." James sucked in a sharp breath. "When they all looked up, they saw the source of the liquid. Bat-like wings, eyes narrow at the corners, stretched to the bottom of their faces, sharp teeth that pushed their lips back into a menacing grin."

"What where they?" Ryan asked when James paused.

"They were the gargoyles, the same ones that are now statues around the Dome. They rained attacks over the Dome until the Vamps were all destroyed. Many of the werewolves fled with the Druids on their backs, yet a lot of them were engulfed in the flames of the gargoyles' burning breath. That was the moment when everyone knew that there was a new enemy, an adversary nobody was prepared to face."

Atlanta glanced at Ryan and flinched at the expression on his face. His eyes were aflame with rage, as if he were living the story her uncle was telling. She could see his muscles ripple with the desire to lash out. She reached out and touched his hand, and when he looked at her his tension eased.

"What about Marcus?" Ryan asked, after giving Atlanta a slight smile. "Where was he in all this?"

James leaned back and cleared his throat. "Some of the vampire elders roamed the city looking for him. It was strange that their leader would desert them in a time like this, and nobody understood what was happening. They finally found him the forests, frozen. His fangs protruding, his eyes open, and his mouth silently roaring with wrath. He was taken back to Calen, and the moment he exited the borders of the forests he was able to move again."

Atlanta stared at her uncle, unable to wrap her head around what had happened. Gargoyles? Frozen Vamps? Who could do this? Witches? They were nearly powerless, weren't they?

"Marcus was told of what had happened to the city, the werewolves being set free and the war that set Calen aflame. He gathered all the vampires and prepared to take the city back, yet before he could he was faced with a threat that he could not have expected, even darker than the gargoyles..." James paused and rubbed his temples with his hands. He slowly looked up. "What Marcus didn't know was that Adelaide had used his blood to create a hybrid more powerful than any being warring in the streets of Calen. It had the form and body of a vampire, coupled with magical powers that gave it an advantage over both vampire and Werewolf. She made more than one. They could compel anyone, even a vampire if needed. So, in a matter of seconds, the remaining vampires turned against each other."

Ryan snorted, but James cut him off before he could speak.

"The same happened in the ranks of the Werewolves and, suddenly, the line between friend and foe had disappeared. Werewolves were slaughtering Druids, and turning against each other. It—"

"I was told a different story," Ryan cut in. "I was told that the night the Druids came to Calen was a time of alliance and peace."

James nodded. "It was a night of alliance, but not peace. The battle with the Vamps soon ceased. Marcus reappeared at the court where the Druids and the heads of the packs were trying to uncover what was happening. His race was less than half its size, and their power undermined by the hybrids. It was at that moment that the warring races grouped to fight the one force none of them could face on their own."

"Why?" Atlanta whispered. "Why would Adelaide do this?"

Her uncle continued, as if he hadn't heard her speak. "The next day, a young witch came to the Druids and offered her help to get rid of the hybrids. She'd escaped Adelaide's claws a long time before and had been in hiding. The Druids escorted her to the palace, where she began working on an enchantment that would lock the hybrids away forever. With the help of Marcus the hybrids were drawn into the palace, where they were outnumbered by the Druids. The battle that followed was one of the worst in Druid history, easily overshadowing the previous days of fighting in Calen. The witch was able to trap the hybrids behind a magical door, the same one we saw back at the Dome." James sighed, looking at both Atlanta and Ryan as their mouths hung open in overwhelming shock. "Peace was established between the families, and the Druids became the protectors of Calen. The door was hidden behind the walls of the palace, and soon the palace was made into the Dome."

Atlanta stared at the bookshelf beside the couch where James was sitting. Her eyes gazed at a maroon- colored book on the shelf, and her mind slowly took in the details of the story. She exchanged looks with Ryan, swallowing the tale, their minds racing at the thought of the hybrids.

But it made sense.

If Louis wasn't murdered by a Werewolf, it was only a hybrid who could have been powerful enough to take him down. It also explained Ryan's attack, and what happened at the football field earlier.

Still, the mere thought of it made her shudder.

Hybrids compelled him, she thought to herself as she fixed her gaze on Ryan's eyes. She suddenly remembered something her uncle had told her back at the Dome. "Wasn't the door closed when you checked?"

"It was, as it has always been," he said, nodding. "Nothing could have escaped."

"But if it wasn't a hybrid that compelled Ryan, then how do we explain all this? Could there be other hybrids?" she asked as she frantically waved her hands around.

"What about Adelaide?" Ryan interfered. "You didn't mention what happened to her."

"That's what I'm afraid of," James replied, pushing himself off the couch and walking towards the them. "No one's heard from Adelaide after what happened to the hybrids. She most likely left Calen, disappeared to some other city, and continued with her wickedness elsewhere. However, until a while after the Insurgence there was still a readiness for the attack of another hybrid. The witch who helped the Druids told them that Adelaide had one hybrid with her wherever she went, a guard of sorts. And after the hybrids were locked up and she disappeared, all feared that she would return with her hybrid to try to disturb the peace again. But years have gone by without anything happening. Everyone's forgotten about Adelaide and the havoc she wreaked."

Atlanta swallowed. She knew deep in her gut that what her ancestors had feared at that time was probably what they were facing now. Adelaide's hybrid, or hybrids, was probably the one who'd killed Louis and the one who'd compelled Ryan to attack them at the Dome. She was about to voice her concerns, when her uncle's eyes widened.

He stared at a distant point, his mouth opening and closing, and then he slowly turned to her. "The people in the field earlier that day, they weren't after Ryan," James said. "Ryan was compelled for the same reason they were. They aren't trying to randomly disturb the peace. They're actually after..."

"The witch who helped the Druids," Atlanta interrupted, suddenly feeling the familiar chill race through her. "Who was she and where did she go?"

James acted like he hadn't heard her. He turned around and looked to the other side, and for a moment it seemed like he wasn't in the same room as them.

"Uncle James!" Atlanta snapped, her voice growing louder and more shaken.

He replied almost dismissively, with a voice so low it was as if he was giving the question no importance. Yet the answer he gave sent a surge of overwhelming shock down Atlanta's bones. "The witch is Beatrice," James replied.

"Who's Beatrice?"

"Your grandmother."

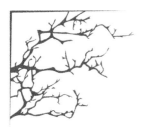

Chapter 12

WHAT?! MY GRANDMOTHER?

The words hit Atlanta like a spell that froze her blood. She'd never seen her grandmother before, yet James had told her stories about her. When Atlanta was young, flailing and falling onto the floor of the training area in the basement, her uncle would pick her up and tell her a story about the one Druid who drove all evil from the city. Yet, as Atlanta grew up, she'd started to think that the stories about Beatrice were a myth created by James for the sole purpose of inspiring her to get up on her feet, and to encourage her to keep training.

Beatrice would also be James' mother, she thought to herself as she stared at the ceiling.

She suddenly remembered all those instances where things out of the ordinary had happened around her uncle. When she was younger she climbed up a tree outside the house, chasing a squirrel that had been eying her all day through the window. She remembered when she flicked the branch of the tree, her foot had slipped and she fell. She remembered closing her eyes, waiting for the sound of bones cracking, her head curled up in her arms. But nothing happened. Her feet had never touched the ground. She had hovered above the ground for at least five seconds, and in her head those five seconds were like an eternity.

It wasn't an illusion, she thought to herself now.

If James' mother was a witch, then her uncle must possess some sort of power.

How had she not realized it before?

It made perfect sense; he saved her from the fall that day. The image grew more and more vivid in her mind as she went through the events at the Dome. She recalled how James was on the floor, unconscious behind her, then suddenly being propelled like a missile towards Marcus and Ryan. She remembered the green glow that surrounded her, and how the next thing she could remember was being in the basement of her house.

"He used magic to transport us," she muttered to herself as she rolled off the bed, her mind in another world completely.

"Well, I wouldn't say magic."

Atlanta yelped and turned around, her heart skipping a beat.

James was standing at the door of her room, arms crossed and a smirk on his face. It seemed like he had been standing there for a while, and she had been none the wiser.

"It was more of a reaction, an instinct to protect," James continued.

"What else are you keeping from me?" Atlanta asked, too tired to be angry, yet frustrated enough to skip pleasantries.

"Listen," James started as he unfolded his arms and looked straight into Atlanta's eyes. "I wouldn't keep anything from you unless it was for your own good. I hope you trust me with that."

"I do, but I think you underestimate how much I can handle," she said dismissively as she walked out the door and left him gazing at her empty bed. She could feel her uncle's eyes on her back, and she made it a point not to turn around as she walked into the bathroom and closed the door. She leaned against it, listening as her uncle's footsteps disappeared down the stairs; only then did she let out a frustrated sigh.

What else was going to come out of the woodwork? She glanced wearily at the wall. *Possibly literally.*

She pushed off from the door and stood in front of the bathroom mirror as she turned on the water. She took a deep breath and realized how much she was dreading the day she had to face. She no longer knew what to expect. The things she then knew about Calen frightened her to her core. The stories she heard about witches were on rare occasions and had always seemed like a myth. But in the course of one night she had found out that the evil that had almost torn Calen apart a century ago, and threatened the lives of many, was a witch.

Not to mention good old Beatrice, Atlanta thought bitterly. *Family tree of witches.*

If James had had some magic powers all along then it was safe to assume that her mother did, too. So why couldn't she escape the fire that had orphaned Atlanta? If her powers could make her transport from one place to the other in the blink of an eye, why didn't she use those powers to save herself?

The surge of tears came welling up in her eyes. She pressed her lips tight. She was not going to think of her parents. It had always been a matter for another day whenever it came to her mind. She could never handle the pain. She had always hated it, the weakness and surrender that came with the agony.

Then, as air escaped her ballooned lungs, she splashed water on her face. The cool liquid washed down the flowing emotions that warmed her cheeks. The tears came with the water. She could breathe easier.

Let it out, she told herself. If only briefly, even if she had to repeat to herself that it was just tap water, that they weren't tears.

A brief silence broke into her mind. The gears of her thoughts cracked and sped up. It was almost as if her consistent thinking was rolling on to lead to this one realization she was now having, and she didn't know if she should grin, or frown, or dwell in fear from herself.

Do I have powers?

Atlanta stood frozen, staring at herself in the mirror. If her mother, James, and Beatrice all had magical powers, then it was only logical that she would have them, too. Then it might not have been her uncle who had saved her from that fall all those years ago. *Could I have done it? Was I the one who floated?*

She opened the door of the bathroom and rushed outside. She had to be sure. She had to know the complete truth. She knew that she had made her uncle feel guilty earlier, but it was the only way she could get anything out of him. She could ask him whatever questions she wanted and he would answer not in words, but in stories.

She ran down the stairs to the living room where she knew her uncle was waiting to take her to school, and from the restlessness of her mind she started speaking way before she had reached him. "Uncle James, I was wondering," she started between slight pants and excitement. "Do I—"

She fell silent at the sight of Marcus standing in the living room with James. He looked like he had just arrived, and before she could utter another word the words came out in his deep, husky voice.

"Colin Toller was murdered last night."

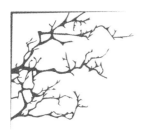

Chapter 13

THE NIGHT BEFORE

James grunted as he carried Atlanta up the stairs to her room and lay her down softly, making sure not to wake her. She'd fallen asleep on the couch in the basement, frustrated and angry when he couldn't give her the answers she was looking for.

He felt like he had already said too much. He knew he couldn't protect her forever, but for now he had to make sure he didn't overwhelm her. He wondered momentarily if he should've told her the truth about the Insurgence a long time ago. It didn't matter. It was too late for what-ifs, and he was far too tired to beat himself up about it now.

When he returned to the basement, Ryan had already put his shirt back on and was looking for his shoes. James had untied him not long after he'd told them the truth about the Insurgence.

"You okay?" James asked.

Ryan shot him a less than friendly glance and nodded slightly. "I need to get home."

"I'll drive you." The wolf in front of him was just a boy, but James knew better.

Ryan snorted. "I could run the distance in seconds. You'll only slow me down."

"Not with those injuries."

Ryan hesitated, and James could see that he was struggling to ask him something. "Spit it out," James coaxed.

"You should have told us before." Ryan glared at him. "You should have told Atlanta."

"I was protecting her."

"One would think that telling her the truth would protect her."

James sighed. "One day, Ryan, you're going to understand what I did and why."

"I doubt it." Ryan grunted and stood up. "Let's go. Please."

THE DOOR TO THE SKOLAR house was dark brown with a brass knob right in the middle. From far away, the sides of the door were in line with the window of Atlanta's room right above it. The window was painted white, black panels on both sides and underneath it. On a regular day it was an inviting scene, one that promised a sanctuary of sorts from the world outside.

However, on that night a dark figure shrouded the top part of the window.

The sun had begun to rise as James and Ryan left the house through the garage. Soft beams of light were beginning to fall on the paneled rooftop, but on the window to Atlanta's room the shade was a crown.

The figure hovered and hung upside down, his head dangling, taking glimpses of her room. His shoulders were broad, arms crossed, and although his head was on the crosshair of the force of gravity the black hood didn't shake or fall from his head. His face was covered with the darkness that accompanied his shadowy figure. Only his fangs shone through his hooded image.

He had been in the orbit of the Skolar house all night, prowling the corners of every window, keeping watch on the one who would save his brothers. He had tried to get into the house several times, pushing open the window to her room. But as his body touched the air inside the house his entire silhouette was repelled, uninvited. The window would glow in invisible green flickers. No matter how many spells he cast, the house still seemed like uncharted area for him.

When James had bolted out of the house on his bike the first time, the dark figure had tried entering through the front door. Yet the moment his feet were a length from the tiles of the entrance his whole body felt paralyzed, cemented and repelled.

And when she'd glimpsed him standing there, he rose from his hypnotized posture and hovered back into his bat-like position by the window of her room.

On the window, next to the door of the house, the raven that accompanied him wherever he went, his 'eye,' stayed, glaring at her. The smallest specks of light in the darkest of rooms were absorbed by the raven's eyes, resting on the focal points in its red-engulfed retina. Yet the image wouldn't form anywhere in its blank mind.

The figure watched James and Ryan leave, and he realized that trying to enter the house again would be useless. Even though the only one in Calen they needed was lying asleep inches away, it felt like his mother would be more satisfied with another disturbance. In his malicious, frosted heart, he knew where to go next.

The engine of James' bike roared and Ryan hopped on behind him. The figure waited until they were at a distance before bolting behind them. His cloaked body jumped from building to building, like a shadow that disappeared at the touch of the walls, dissipating and reappearing at the edge of another building. The towers of Calen rose to slap at the sky as he followed the fumes coming from James' bike.

A few minutes later, a house with dark grey walls came into view. The white rooftop was divided into two triangles, the one on the right nearly half the size of the other. The one on the left had a circular window that almost looked like a porthole, and on the two sides of the paneled triangle that shaped a room were two other porthole-like windows. Their purpose was to focus all the light coming in from the moon, to invite it in from any direction as it hung proudly in the sky. The figure knew the house. The room under the bigger triangle was Colin's.

The figure dangled from a tree, both legs slightly touching a branch, almost as if he was attached to the tree through a peculiar force of gravity. From far away he looked like a shadow under the shade of a tree, camouflaged. He watched Ryan slip painfully off the motorbike, and waited as the men below talked briefly. James' lips moved, then there was a moment of silence. James patted Ryan on the side of his arm; Ryan smiled and then turned to the house.

The bike thundered away but the birds in the trees didn't move. The figure was pulling them towards him, not from the nature of his being but to keep the air silent and the fierce eyes of the werewolves away from the moving branches.

When Ryan entered the house, the figure descended from his position in the tree. He glared at the room under the triangular roof on the left, and in a swift movement his legs bent and stretched to reappear yards ahead, on top of the roof. Not a sound was made, not a single panel on the roof breathed, his movements as silent as the sound of the sinking moon.

Through the window he could see the room clearly. The sunbeams rested on a corner table right across from the bed. The figure gazed a moment at the picture of Ryan with his father. *Colin*, he hissed. In the picture it looked like they were on a mountaintop, a vastness of white clouds and greenery behind them.

His eyes slowly investigated the rest of the room. He sensed a heaviness weighing down the bed. It was covered in blankets. The figure twisted, trying to get a better view. From where he hovered, the top side of the bed couldn't be seen. He moved swiftly, and reappeared on the other side of the room to look in that window. A set of pillows covered in blankets rested where a sleeping body should have been.

The figure squinted and his fangs elongated, his body glowing with a slight mist of green. But before he could even turn back or begin to investigate the rest of the house, a deep and long howl sent the birds around the house in search of the sun. He was bombarded with a heavy collision from behind. Sharp teeth pierced his neck and claws dug deep into the back of his shoulders as they fell, rolling in a heap on the wet grass behind the house.

The figure's head snapped up. Colin had fully turned, much larger than most werewolves, a black-furred beast with eyes that were as yellow as the flaming sun. He growled as he pinned down the now-unhooded figure and tore part of his skin from the back of his neck.

No blood seeped out from the intruder, and when Colin's claws dug deep into his back he didn't even cry out.

He was being crushed under Colin's enormous weight. A bite in the neck from a Werewolf like Colin usually meant instant fatality, yet for this one the damage did little more than stun him.

Colin went for another snap with his jowls, but was suddenly biting the grass. The figure under him disappeared, as if he'd liquefied and then seeped through Colin's fierce claws.

He nearly laughed as Colin turned around, growling at him standing just out of the wolf's reach. He watched the wolf stare at his human face. The sky of his eyes was black, not white, and in the middle the redness of them alternated hues when his fangs elongated. His forehead was covered with his light brown hair, falling on his face like a veil, like the way his hood usually did. He shrugged his broad shoulders. The rest of his body was abnormally slim, his cloak usually hiding that as well.

As Colin stared, the figure laughed as he suddenly sent the green mist surrounding him flowing toward the wolf.

Colin leaped, trying to attack the figure again. Halfway through the air, he shifted.

The figure watched, his face expressionless. He knew what was happening inside the wolf. Pain raced through its body, and through it the wolf could feel his fur recede back into his skin, changing color quickly. His fangs shrank back into teeth and the sharpness of them dissipated into the light of the day. And when he was inches away from falling headfirst on the attacker, his eyes changed from the wrathful flaming yellow into the deep brown color of his human form.

He fell straight into the hands of the figure standing in front of him, grinning.

Claws held Colin from the back of his neck as the figure slammed his face into the ground. The figure lifted him up again with ease, as if picking up a doll.

Colin tried to growl, probably tried to shift, but all that came out was a crackly sigh.

The figure bent his head to a side, taking in the look on Colin's worn face. A raven descended on the attacker's shoulders and stared at Colin with glaring red eyes.

With his other hand, the figure buried his claws in Colin's chest, penetrating the ribcage. Colin gasped as the hand withdrew, ripping his heart out. His heart pounded for a few seconds before turning to ash, and the figure dropped Colin, lifeless, on the ground.

The attacker stared at what was left of the shifter for a few seconds before turning his head to gaze at the smaller triangular rooftop of Ryan's room.

The raven soared from his shoulders and turned to face him. Through the simultaneousness of purpose and the blankness of his mind, he knew what to do next.

The figure soared into the air, disappearing just as Ryan raced out of the house. Looking behind him, he watched Ryan fall to his knees, holding his father's devoured body and howling in rage at the morning sky.

Things were about to get very interesting in Calen.

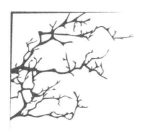

Chapter 14

PRESENT DAY

Atlanta sighed for the millionth time. Through the window of the car, the skies bent down in a grey melancholy blur that flattened the thoughts in her mind. And like the skies, her silence and grief hung like a heavy shroud over her. She barely glanced at her uncle as they drove home from the funeral, but it was clear he was just as devastated as she was. She knew how far back her uncle and Colin had gone.

They were high school buddies. Like me and Ryan.

The only difference was that there was way more history between James and Colin, and Atlanta had a hard time wrapping her head around how her uncle must feel. The frown on his face said a lot about his anger, but what worried her more was that he wasn't showing any grief.

Anger didn't lead to the smartest way of thinking. He'd taught her that.

He's mad at what killed Colin. Wants to find it. Probably tear its guts out.

Atlanta had eavesdropped on her uncle speaking with one of the Werewolf elders. It was apparent from Colin's body that he'd been killed in the same way Louis had been. The signs were obvious. Without a doubt, it was the same attacker. The news would circulate around Calen, and soon there would be the outrage of misled werewolves who immediately blamed the Vamps, a form of revenge for Louis' murder. It was one of the reasons that it was important for Marcus to be at the funeral, talking with the elders, sharing his concern and vowing to do what must be done.

"What happens now?" Atlanta asked, looking over at her uncle and blinking back the tears that had started to form in her eyes.

James shook his head and didn't reply. There had been talk about the urgency in need of guarding the door in the Dome and, most importantly, finding a new leader for the pack.

It was a subject her Uncle James was deliberately ignoring.

"What about Ryan?" Atlanta asked, not referring to the new leader issue but something else entirely.

James gave her a quick look before returning his attention to the road in front of them. They'd found Colin's body, but there was no sign of Ryan anywhere. James was the last one to see the boy when he dropped him off at his house, and that only meant one of two things. Either Ryan was dead, or he'd been taken by the same beast who'd killed his father. No matter what the explanation was his disappearance had to be sorted out, especially with the leaders of the other packs hungrily circling the Toller territory, blood- thirsty and willing to disturb the peace they had all been working so hard to maintain.

"Uncle James?"

"Not now, Atlanta," James cut her short. "We'll figure this out later."

LATER TOOK A LOT LONGER than either of them expected.

Days went by with no sign of Ryan. Several meetings were held at the Dome, where wolves and vampires argued endlessly. Atlanta had been adamant on attending each and every one of them, and she watched as James interfered almost every time with a calm and rational solution to each problem. It was impressive to see him do what he did, but Atlanta knew it was only a matter of time before his words held no meaning. The rage was bottling up on both sides, and she knew her uncle was only prolonging an inevitable collision that would set the city aflame.

"Do you think he's dead?" she blurted out one day as they drove back from the Dome, turning her eyes from the corner of the passenger window and to the distance in the road ahead. She'd tried looking for Ryan, and was stopped each night by her uncle. He didn't want her out on her own, after dark or during the day. It was beginning to feel like a prison. She pushed her thoughts aside and told herself to focus on finding Ryan. And nothing else.

"I doubt that," he replied after a moment of thought. "If he were dead, his body would've been found by now."

"What makes you sure of that?" she asked as her mind struggled to paint her pain in words.

"I'm almost sure that Louis and Colin's killer is a hybrid," he declared, "and if so, then they wouldn't kill anyone without leaving his body behind. They'd want to make a scene. Try to upset the peace."

"Then where is he?" she demanded desperately.

"When I talked to Marcus, we reached the conclusion that Ryan has probably gone somewhere in the forests or the mountains, somewhere he and Colin would usually go," he sighed. "The werewolves usually go to places as silent and calm as the mountains to learn to control their anger. We think he's gone off on his own. That he's not been taken."

He looked at her, and she fought to stop the surge of tears that was eating her composure alive. He held her hand to console her, but she instantly pulled it away and again gazed out the window, hiding the tears that rolled down her cheeks. "You're just saying that to make me feel better."

James inhaled a long breath and let it out slowly. "I've always believed Ryan was smarter than his father. When Colin grew angry, he would fight to control it in until it burst out like wildfire. More than once, he nearly turned in public. He couldn't control it." He chuckled, clearly remembering something Atlanta didn't know. His face turned serious again as the memory passed. "Surprisingly, he taught his son not to be like that. Colin was a leader, I won't argue that. He learned to control his anger as he got older. But when he was Ryan's age...he was different. Colin tried to teach Ryan to find ways to control the anger. I know he wanted that for his son. He wanted Ryan to have a better chance, do a better job than he did. Maybe he knew that one day the leadership would fall into Ryan's hands. Maybe he hoped it would." He waved his hand. "It doesn't matter. What I think, and I'm not saying this to make you feel hope—or feel better—I think Ryan knew that the loss of his father would make him react fiercely. He knows that the wrong reaction could upset the peace. Or make him a victim right beside his father. I think he understood this, so he took off to the mountains to compose his feelings."

"Maybe." Atlanta clenched her jaw tight, unable to say more. She was both sad and furious. They drove the rest of the way home in silence.

By the time James pulled up to the house the sun was out of sight, leaving room for dusk to sit in its throne for the night. She looked down right before she got out of the car, wiped away the tears that were reaching her chin, and then turned her face to her uncle.

James was gazing at the purple sky behind their house. "Look at the sky," he whispered. "It's a full moon. When it begins to split and the dark side takes over the bright one, I bet you Ryan will be back."

"I hope so," she replied, dismissive of the attempt to reassure her as she got out the car. "I'm heading to the basement."

James nodded absently as they headed into the house.

Atlanta's mind overflowed with worry about what could possibly happen next. The Wolves and Vamps were at the edge of falling into a war that could threaten the existence of both races in the city.

Yet that was only a fraction of the fear that filled her mind. If her uncle's stories were true, then the murders that had happened and the hybrid who'd suddenly appeared in Calen could only add up to one thing.

Someone was trying to open the door.

She left her uncle in the hallway and made her way to the basement. *I need to think. Someone has to figure this out before it's too late. I need time alone.*

She dropped down onto the couch and thought about the night Ryan had been there. All she could think about was him, and what his continued disappearance meant for her and for Calen.

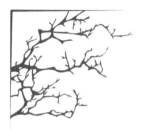

Chapter 15

THE SAND COMPRESSED inside the rubber bags as the sound of the pounding reverberated in the basement again and again. Atlanta grunted as anger oozed out of her like oxygen escaping. She couldn't stop panting or sweating; she ignored her lungs' cry for more air and her body's feeling of exhaustion. She kicked another sandbag and forced her eyes to stay open. Sweat sucked into her crimson red suit and she knew her hair had gone wild from the constant spinning and practice attacks.

She turned towards the bars and poles that hung horizontally and vertically around the vast basement, and leapt from one pole to the other, her body in perfect rhythm with her mind's commands. Strands of her brown hair fell on her forehead as she dangled upside-down from a pole in the corner. The fluorescent lights beamed in hues of white and light blue, casting a weird light against her shadow.

It was well after midnight when James had come down and started altering the mechanics of the bike. His brow was furrowed in concentration and Atlanta can see how his muscles flexed as he worked, as if he were focusing all his feelings into action. He was working on a table that had a bow arched and framed with silver. The arrows had a sharp marble edge on top of them that glowed with green light, different from any light that emerged from the heart of a stone.

He's trying too hard, Atlanta thought as she watched him. *He's going to lose it.*

James suddenly slammed his hands on the table, slightly, as if to make sure he would save up some of his anger for later. He frowned and growled in frustration. His eyes closed as sweat rolled down his face, and he swept away a tear that had tried to escape. He rolled his eyes up to the ceiling, and when he caught her watching he turned and went back to work.

Atlanta felt a shudder race through her. Her uncle was always composed; seeing him like this brought out a vulnerability she wasn't accustomed to. He was always her rock when the world stopped making sense, and for the first time in forever she caught glimpse of what it meant for the both of them to be overwhelmed.

We need to be strong for each other. Somehow. She closed her eyes and listened to the slightest sounds around her: the clanking of tools, the whistling wind outside, the creaks of the house resting. An image of Ryan formed behind her closed lids, and it took every ounce of strength not to falter. She missed him. A lot.

"Atlanta?"

She opened her eyes and gazed at her uncle. There was a moment of silence before she pulled her upper body upwards and her arms waved to touch her feet. She held onto the bar and slid her legs until her feet softly touched the floor.

Ever since her parents died, Atlanta's reaction to being emotionally overwhelmed in any way was one of two mechanisms. She would sometimes stay in the basement for days and nights, detached from the outside world. Her only solace and escape was the pounding of the sand bags and the sound of the knives piercing the boards. However, if she had to be outside of the house, her mind would drift. The sound of lips moving and uttering sounds that mingled into conversation sounded more like the sound of two metals pressing against one another. Even James hardly approached her until he would find a hole in her armor and strike up a random conversation.

Which was why his attempt to talk to her right now was odd and out of place.

That's never a good thing.

"Easy there," James said quietly. "Don't be too hard on yourself."

"Maybe all I've been lately is too easy on myself," Atlanta muttered. "I've been nothing but a useless sidekick since the beginning of all this."

"There was nothing we could've done," he replied instantly. "We couldn't have helped Louis or Colin."

"That night when we came back from the Dome," she uttered under her sigh. She slid her back down the wall and sat down on the floor, her knees folded and her face buried in her lap. "Ryan told me he'd seen a raven staring at him from the window in his room right before he woke up in the basement. The last memory he had was of the raven. And I made fun of him, thought he was trying to make a joke in the middle of the chaos that was our day." She paused and swallowed, trying to stop the racing of her heart.

"That doesn't make this your fault—"

"When I went upstairs to find the bandages," she interrupted him, "the door was open, and I could've sworn I saw someone standing there. Like a hooded shadow. But it was there for a moment and then vanished, and all that remained was a raven just like the one Ryan mentioned. That must mean something." She looked up at her uncle, her face streaked with tears, then buried her face back in between her knees again and said, "And I just ignored it. I don't know why, but I thought it was all in my head."

"What color were the raven's eyes?"

Atlanta's head shot up. *Really? That's what you're taking away from this?* She wanted to scream at him. But the serious look on his face made her freeze. "I don't know, I couldn't see its eyes in the dark," she replied. "But I remember Ryan said something about the ravens having a red glow in their eyes, like the one I saw in the field that day." The beginning of a realization rose in the back of her mind and raced forward, waving to be noticed.

Her uncle stared at her, his mouth hanging open.

"Do you think," she paused for seconds and fell into contemplation. "I remember you said something about ravens in the story about

Adelaide and the Insurgence. Does that have to do with what's happening now?"

"Atlanta," he said, and his voice sank into a tone of confession, "there's something you need to know."

"What?" She grew cold with dread.

"When we went to the Dome, there was no way the door could've been open."

"Then why did we go?" she asked in confusion.

"The thing is," he replied, clearly struggling to get the burden of the truth off his shoulder, "there's only one person who could open the door." He paused and looked at her. "When Beatrice locked the hybrids behind it, they were trapped inside and the key to their escape was with her. The spell she put on it could only be undone by her."

"I don't get what the door has to do with all this, then." Atlanta frowned. "It's closed."

"I know, and that's exactly what they're trying to change," James replied. "If the murders were committed by the one hybrid that accompanied Adelaide when she fled from Calen, then he must be back to free the rest of the hybrids."

"But Grandma died a long time ago. Doesn't that mean that the door is closed for good?"

James sighed before he breathed out the words that put the scattered pieces in her mind into one clear explanation. "No, it isn't. The spell could then be undone by Beatrice, and when she died your mother was the only one who could do the same." He hesitated, waiting for a reaction, before finally saying, "And now you're the one who possesses that power."

Atlanta felt her entire world shatter around her. For a moment she felt like she was being thrown into a dark room, its door closing with a slam and a key turning to lock it from the outside. Her breath caught in her chest, and her heart skipped a beat, and then another. "What?" she managed to croak.

"The power to open the door," James repeated, "now belongs to you."

She felt the blood rush from her face. "Me?"

James nodded.

"I have...powers?"

James smiled, but it wasn't a happy gesture. He looked more like he was trying to comfort her, like he almost pitied her.

"I'm a witch?"

James quickly shook his head. "Don't think of it like that."

"How else am I supposed to think of it?" Atlanta blurted, rage building inside her like a torrent of fire racing through her veins.

"Atlanta—"

"When were you going to tell me?" Atlanta interrupted, her voice rising. "Oh, wait, let me guess. You were protecting me!"

James winced and averted his eyes, grimacing as he tried to control his own temper. "This wasn't an easy decision," he finally said. "I needed the right time to tell you, and this definitely is not it. In light of what's happening, I don't have much choice."

"So you were never going to tell me?"

James sighed. "Of course I was."

"Like hell!" she screamed, and before her uncle could say anything else she stormed up the basement stairs then slammed the door behind her.

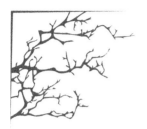

Chapter 16

THE SUN ROSE ON A NEARBY part of the city. She was sleeping under a willow tree that kept the morning sun from her pale white skin. Her long strands of black hair fell around her curled-up body. She slept with her head leaned back and legs folded, her lips aligned like two crescent moons that hugged. A single strand of green hair fell on her forehead, then on the side of her chin. Birds were cracking melodies that fell uneasy on her sleeping mind. Her eyes slowly opened and the tunnels of evergreen lingered in her dilating pupils. She forced the frown away with a single long blink of her eyes and breathed in the breeze that circled the ancient tree behind her.

Skylar's house was close to Atlanta's. It was a fairly small house with a willow tree that stood for decades before she set foot in her new home. From the window of her room, Skylar could see the forests stepping down to the hills far away. Her room wasn't ordinary. Stacks of old books were on the shelves and in every dust- filled corner. The sunlight could barely find its way into her room, the windows halfway tinted with a dark blue cover. Yet she rarely slept in the room.

She and her stepbrother Michael had lived in the decaying walls of the house for nearly seven years on their own. They moved to Calen when their parents had decided to embark on a journey to Europe ten years before, and had left them with their late grandmother. But after six months, they learned their parents weren't coming back, having found a house by the sea in Mikonos. Shortly after, Skylar and Michael received a letter informing them that their parents had died in a fire.

When that happened, Skylar was only eleven years old and her brother nine. She'd handled it relatively well, taking care of her brother and herself. She'd even taken it upon herself to make sure they were both keeping up with their education. The stacks of books that paraded through their house were carved in the deepest part of her memories, the words and metaphors constantly in her rambling thoughts.

Still, it was a lonely life. Until she met Atlanta. Friends since the seventh grade, they were similar in many ways. Neither was keen on socializing and mostly kept to themselves. Their eccentricity made it hard for them to talk to each other earlier than when they did, but once they got past the initial awkwardness that eccentricity drew them closer to each other.

Skylar still remembered the first time they had to work on a project together. Their similarities stunned them when they realized they shared the same interest in books, and their favorite reads were nearly the same. Their obsession with literature made them create a sort of ether that swayed their conversations and their friendship as a whole. But what really marked the deep emotional connection they had with each other was the fact that they had both lost their parents in a fire.

It was time to wake up and get moving.

Skylar stood after a night of sleeping outside by the tree and softly walked towards the house. She hadn't talked to Atlanta at all for the past three weeks. She was bothered by Atlanta's detachment at times, but what irritated her was not that her best friend was far away from her. She related to Atlanta's detachment, knowing that when it happened it was usually because something serious was happening with her.

She took out her phone and Atlanta's name flashed on the screen. Surprised, she quickly tapped on the answering button and held the phone to her ear. "Look who finally remembered my existence!" she exclaimed cheerfully.

From the other end of the call, there was only silence.

"Atlanta?" Skylar looked at the phone's screen again, noticing Atlanta had hung up before she'd even heard Skylar's words. She tried calling again but Atlanta wouldn't answer, which only stirred her worry even more. Usually when Atlanta would suddenly disappear, Skylar knew to give her enough space to regain her composure. Usually she would start talking on her own. But this time, it had been nearly a month since they had last seen each other or talked.

Something's off. Skylar decided against going to school and walked to her silver sedan in the driveway. *If Atlanta won't talk, then I'll get the answers myself.*

She opened the door and sat in the car for a moment, suddenly doubting her decision. Shaking her head, she decided Atlanta might never come out of this one, and was probably in dire need of a friend more than ever. She turned the key and welcomed the roar of the engine.

Listening to the engine instead of music, she drove toward to the Skolars' house. When she arrived, she idled in the driveway and gazed up at the window of Atlanta's room.

Atlanta was standing by the curtains, staring out into space, oblivious that her best friend had just arrived.

Skylar stepped out of the car and waved at her repeatedly, but it was almost as if she were invisible.

Earth to Atlanta, she wanted to scream, but knew it was useless. Atlanta was gone, and from the look of it, far, far away. She wouldn't notice Skylar even if she were accompanied by an entire marching band. She made her way to the front door and rang the doorbell, taking a step back to look up Atlanta again. She rang the bell again, and James opened the door.

"Good morning, Mr. Skolar," Skylar said, smiling as the sun paraded around her deep green eyes

"Hey there, Skylar, come on in," James replied. "Where've you been? Haven't seen you in a while."

"I've been around," she said as she walked into the house. "Atlanta's the one who's been distant lately. I barely catch her in school."

"She's been a bit in her head lately," he replied instantly. "How's Michael?"

"Nothing new. He hardly leaves the house anymore. I finally got him to read though," Skylar said with enthusiasm.

"That's wonderful to hear," James replied, flashing her a smile but looking distracted himself.

Skylar turned when she heard footsteps on the stairs, and a few seconds later Atlanta appeared. She wore a strange smile, one that Skylar immediately knew was fake, and her eyes seemed darker than usual. If there was one thing she knew about Atlanta, it was that you could read her emotions like an open book. And right now, her friend was hurting. Really hurting.

It's almost as if she hasn't slept in days. Skylar hesitated for only a moment before she rushed over to Atlanta and hugged her. She could feel the other girl melt in her arms, as if she were carrying a heavy weight that was too much to bear alone.

"I'll leave you two and go make some breakfast," James said as he smiled and moved towards the kitchen. "Skylar, you hungry?"

"No thanks, Mr. Skolar; I had breakfast right before I left the house," she replied politely. Better to lie than eat James Skolar's cooking.

"Just don't burn the kitchen down, please," Atlanta said then turned back to Skylar, putting the fake smile on again. "How've you been?" Atlanta said as they sat down on the couch by the living room window. "What've you been up to?" She didn't mention that she'd barely been to school the past month, but Skylar had a pretty good idea what Atlanta was referring to.

"Not much," she replied, playing along with Atlanta's fake merriment, giving her friend the space she needed to breathe before pushing her to spill. "I finally finished reading *To Kill a Mockingbird*, and you were right. I think I was missing out on a lot."

"You think? It's a classic! Everything that comes out of Atticus Finch's mouth is a literary jewel," Atlanta exclaimed.

"I know, I loved every single part of the book," Skylar said softly.

There was a moment of silence that followed, even though they had a lot to catch up on.

Atlanta gazed out the window.

"I saw you standing at your bedroom window when I pulled in," Skylar said, trying to break the silence. "I waved, but it was like you weren't there at all." *That should get her talking.*

"I'm sorry," Atlanta replied. "I really didn't see you. You know me when I'm drifting. I daydream a lot." She let out a brief laugh.

Not buying it. "Daydreaming? Yeah, right. I'm beginning to think you seriously need a hobby, something other than gazing out your window."

Atlanta laughed the comment away, and for a moment her eyes almost robotically moved to gaze out the window again.

"So, is there something you want to tell me?" Skylar whispered as she squinted her eyes and waved her hands in front of Atlanta.

"No, not really," Atlanta replied, startled and obviously reaching for some sort of explanation Skylar knew wouldn't be satisfactory. "I just haven't been feeling well lately."

"Something's wrong," Skylar said, shaking her head. "I can see it. You don't simply disappear for this long and then tell me nothing's wrong. I know you, Atlanta, and this is the first time since seventh grade that we've spent a whole month without a word." Skylar's tone was loaded with confusion and worry.

"It's not a month." Atlanta swallowed and glanced out the window. "Just three weeks."

Skylar watched as her friend alternated between looking at her and out the window. "Atlanta? What's going on? Does this have something to do with Ry—"

She gasped when Atlanta grabbed her hand and pulled her off the couch. She found herself being guided out of the living room hurriedly, then rushed up the stairs. Once they were in Atlanta's room, her friend closed the door and leaned against it.

"Skylar, what I'm going to tell you now has to stay between us," Atlanta said assertively, her eyes fixed on Skylar's. "No one can know that you know this. I can't believe I'm telling you."

"What is it? You're freaking me out here, and since when am I a talker?"

"Even Uncle James can't know about this; Michael, too. Literally no one," Atlanta said, her voice growing more assertive. More desperate.

"I won't tell a soul." Whatever was going on with her best friend, it was bad. Was she sick? Cancer? Oh crap, was she pregnant? Skylar shook her head. She doubted the last one. That didn't make sense.

"I don't know where to start," Atlanta said, trying to gather her thoughts. "Just don't hate me for hiding this from you."

"Are you pregnant?"

"No, of course not! That's what you're thinking?" Atlanta responded mockingly. "Now you're making it even harder for me explain what's been going on." She stood from the bed and went back beside the window, then frantically moved towards the bookshelf and back.

Skylar sat on the bed, her mind swirling in black holes of confusion.

"Look, I'll just tell you everything," Atlanta blurted. "I haven't been honest with you about many things in my life, and it isn't because I don't trust you; it's just that it's against the rules of the Hand to talk to an ordinary about the nature of this city."

She's been lying to me? "Ordinary?" Skylar interrupted. "Hand? This sounds like a lame part of a fantasy sequel." She laughed.

"You're not far off with that guess." Atlanta sighed and closed her eyes. "Just keep an open mind. Please."

Skylar waited, leaning on her knees, but before Atlanta could utter a word James opened the door.

"Sorry to barge in, girls," James said, forcing a smile at Skylar before turning to Atlanta. "I need to talk to you. Now."

Skylar smiled awkwardly as Atlanta shot her a glance and disappeared outside, closing the door behind them. She strained to hear what they were talking about, but their voices were too low and muffled.

Ten minutes later, Atlanta walked back in. The color had returned to her face and her smile suddenly seemed a lot more genuine.

"What happened?" Skylar asked. "Everything okay?"

Atlanta shook her head, then began to cry.

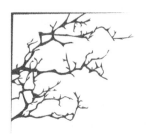

Chapter 17

HE'S BACK. I JUST GOT a call. Ryan's home.

"Atlanta! What's going on?" Skylar's voice rose in panic.

"I'm s-sorry." Atlanta smiled through her tears. "It's okay. Everything's fine." *Well, kind of.*

"What the heck's going on?" Skylar set her hands on her hips and her mouth drew into that thin line she did when she was frustrated and not sure what to do.

"Ryan. He's back. He's okay."

"Ryan? That's why you're crying?" Skylar tilted her head to the side. "Have you got a crush on him?"

"What?" Atlanta wiped her cheeks and started laughing. "No! No. That's not why...oh, forget it." She grabbed Skylar and hugged her. "It's going to be okay. Everything's going to be okay."

Her friend groaned and pushed free of the tight hug. "I'm not so sure. I think you're going looney."

Uncle James tapped on the door again and popped his head in. "Ladies, everything okay in here?" He shot Atlanta a warning look that disappeared a second later. "I've made breakfast. Who's hungry?"

Skylar glanced at Atlanta before turning back to James. "I'm good. Thanks for the offer, though. I need to, uh, get going and check on my brother."

"Your loss." Uncle James winked and headed down the hall, whistling. He'd left the door open and Skylar made her way to it.

"So, you're good?" she asked Atlanta. "You're coming back to school tomorrow?"

Atlanta nodded. "Yeah. I promise. I'll be there."

"Awesome. 'Cause I'm not eating any of your uncle's cooking if I don't have to."

They both burst out laughing.

ATLANTA LAY IN HER bed later that night, staring at the ceiling, her eyes wide, unable to sleep. Her uncle's words resonated inside her mind.

"I just got a call. Ryan's home."

She rolled onto her side and wrapped her arms around her shoulders. She felt like crying all over again, a rush of relief racing through her every time she thought about Ryan's return. She hadn't wanted to say it out loud, but a part of her had believed he was dead. She hated herself for thinking it, but her mind had a way of jumping to the worst.

He's back. He's really back.

She felt her cheeks flush.

She remembered the shock on her friend's face when she had walked back into the room and burst into tears. Atlanta welcomed the other girl's embrace, and really let the waterworks go.

I was going to tell her everything.

She suddenly sat up.

She was going to tell Skylar how her broken arm from last summer wasn't actually because she was sleepwalking and fell down the staircase. She was going to tell her about the time her Uncle James woke her in the middle of the night, and they both stormed to the forest just outside of Calen to fight vampires that were attacking from a nearby town.

I was going to break a vow. How could I be so stupid?

Skylar had pressed her for questions and luckily Uncle James had come in and offered breakfast, saving Atlanta from blurting out secrets she had sworn to keep.

When she'd called Skylar earlier in the morning she realized she wasn't ready to lie to her about how she felt, and hung up before she could talk. Then when Skylar showed up at the house she told herself that it was alright, she could handle Skylar, but she never expected her friend to be so blunt. Atlanta had felt cornered. And she wanted to tell Skylar something.

She couldn't explain why, but after everything it seemed like she had no proper reason to hide anything from Skylar. That the sworn to secrecy thing didn't apply to the two of them. She trusted Skylar. She knew Skylar would go to the grave with a secret if Atlanta asked her to. If anything, she would be of help when needed. She thought of the many times she wished she'd told Skylar about her nights spent slaying the rogue vampires. She smiled to herself at the thought of the them spending days drinking coffee and talking about the details of those fights just like they discussed what lay between the lines of every Dostoevsky novel.

Suddenly, the decision was made.

She couldn't take it anymore, the bottled-up emotions that were swelling in her every vein and boiling in the coldest compartments of her head. She was too used to pretending to be all right. And in her friendship with Skylar, especially since it was one based on relating on an emotional level, it got harder with every passing day.

Atlanta sighed and rolled onto her back. She hadn't noticed how much her secret life was taking a toll on her. She was starting to get sloppy, which was a dangerous thing if it meant sharing her secrets. Even if it was Skylar.

How did I let this happen?

She was thankful James had intervened, and with that thought she smiled. The moment she'd heard the words come out of her uncle's mouth, her heart threatened to burst from her chest. The doubts that had engulfed her mind rested like embers that fell around trees in perfect circles. Her body relaxed for the first time in days, and her bottled-up tears rushed back to the locked compartments of her heart, knowing that Ryan hadn't faced the same fate his father did.

Until the moment she closed her eyes and drifted into the one complete cycle of sleep in all the sleepless nights that preceded, she was resisting the urge to go knock on Ryan's door and see for herself that he was back and safe. But she knew it was best to let this one night pass and wait until she saw him in school.

He's back. That's all that matters.

BEFORE DAWN BURST INTO the night, and before the birds sang in the morning, the ravens croaked and rain fell through the silent darkness. Atlanta slowly opened her eyes and blinked, letting the blur of the night sharpen as her eyelashes flexed apart. Her room wasn't its usual mess, especially since she had used up all her anxious and forlorn thoughts into tidying every corner of it. The books were in alphabetical order, her clothes in the wardrobe were a perfect reflection of the spectrum of dispersed white light. Her feet softly swept the sheets as she tried to get out bed.

Her throat was dry and her head ached. Her legs and feet were sore, as if she had run a marathon the day before. Her heart felt heavy, then grew heavier at the sight of the moon obscured at a distance through her window. She heard a raven croak, then the croaking echoed louder and louder. Soon it sounded like a conspiracy of ravens approaching her, but she couldn't tell from where. It was almost as if the croaking wasn't coming from outside, but more as if it were inside her wardrobe. She rushed towards it and slid its veneer doors open. The sound grew louder; it was closer than the fears inside her own head. She threw out all her perfectly folded clothes, yet nothing was there.

Where's it coming from? The throbbing of her heart was an echo of the drizzling rain outside, and all she could see or feel was a blur of what was real.

She stopped frantically throwing her clothes around. She straightened her back and took a deep breath. She locked the air inside her chest and closed her eyes for a second, then exhaled. She turned her back to the closet and looked at the window, and froze.

That's impossible.

There was a branch of a tree sloping from the porch to the window of her room, but she knew it had never been there before. The closest greenery other than the grass of their small garden was yards away. She walked slowly towards the window, eyes fixed on one leaf that was quivering on the branch.

Suddenly her gaze was met with the red eyes of a raven. It croaked as it descended on the branch.

"Get away!" she hissed, and slammed the window with her hands, hoping to scare bird away, but it didn't budge. It stayed put, eyes glaring at her, the redness of their glow growing more and more intense with every shiver that ran through her body. The sound of the croaks suddenly intensified. She turned to look at the closet, in fear that the sound was as close physically as it was in her head. There was still nothing, and when she looked back at the window the raven was gone.

As was the branch.

She leaned closer towards the window and looked down at the porch, but saw nothing. No sign of a raven or the branch; it had all disappeared. She opened the window and looked to both sides of the house, the pounding of her heart slowly easing. *Maybe I'm losing it. Was I dreaming?*

"Ryan's home. That's all that matters," she whispered and took a deep breath, trying to calm her frayed nerves. She slipped her hand outside the window and opened it, palm up to see if it was still raining. Though the sound of the drizzling had ceased, there were still tiny drops falling. She kept her hand outside and her tension dissipated with the coldness of the falling water.

Then, suddenly, the rain intensified. The wind picked up, and she could see the distant trees dancing to its harmony. Her body stopped shivering, her heartbeat's rate was returning to normal, but her feeling of uneasiness wouldn't go away.

She heard an echo of a croak from afar, but dismissed it until she heard it again and closer. Then again. She pulled her hands back in and shook her head, trying to disperse the sounds she was certain were only in her head. But they only grew louder. And louder. So loud she could barely think.

She held the handle of the window with her right arm and pulled the metal-framed window towards her, and once it was closed the croaks disappeared.

She sighed and turned to grab some clothes. It was time to talk to Uncle James. See if he knew what was going on.

She froze when the sound of her window cracking echoed in the room.

Atlanta turned around slowly, her eyes widening, and a silent scream hissed out of her mouth. Talons slammed against the glass. Dozens of ravens fell on her window, crashing against it, the cracks on the glass spreading with every flutter of wings. It was a cacophony of melancholy croaks and the darkest spectrum of black feathers and red eyes.

Run!

Atlanta broke into a sprint just as the window behind her shattered. She ran towards the door, only looking back once at the red eyes glaring at her. She turned back towards the door of her room, but it had transformed, taller and wider, its color now a dark brown.

She hesitated for only a split second, unable to comprehend what she was seeing, then rushed forward and tried opening it.

Locked!

She leaned her back to the red wall surrounding the door. The ravens were all around her now, a bombardment of wings and talons and croaks.

She closed her eyes and screamed. Her cries echoed all around her, and she thrashed against the wings slapping her face.

Then, suddenly, they were gone.

She fell to the floor, her hands still raised to protect her face, and only when she was sure that she was no longer under attack she dropped them. She cautiously opened her eyes, taking in her surroundings.

She was in the Dome.

Someone laughed, and her head snapped in the direction of the sound.

A dark figure stood watching her. His fangs dropped from the sides of his mouth like the sharpened, frozen edges of the caves in the coldest mountains. He wore a hood that shrouded the features of his face. His claws were bloody, so much like the red glare that lined the core of his eyes.

Atlanta felt the world around her begin to swim out of focus. The small distance between her lids narrowed, and all that remained was the redness of his eyes in the background of the blur. Soon, even that began to fade, and slowly melted into darkness.

Her eyes fluttered open a second later. She was back in her room!

She jumped out of bed, the air trapped in her lungs struggling to escape. She shook, and her hands and feet were clenched. *What had happened?* Her gaze tore to the window. Closed and unbroken. Her closet hadn't been touched, and the room was as organized as it had been when she'd fallen asleep.

It was a bad dream.

Finally, the air seeped from between her lips and through the contracted pathways in her nose. The nightmare had passed, but she couldn't shake the image of the hooded man that remained etched at the forefront of her mind.

Chapter 18

THE MORNING SUN GLEAMED through the window of Atlanta's room as she struggled to get out of bed. Every time she shifted closer to the edge of her mattress her eyes closed, and her mind sought warmth in dark silence, then another nightmare would come parading with melancholy vividness.

She stayed under the covers, turning from side to side, trying to escape the morning sun. She needed more sleep after the marathon of dreams that came crashing to her during the night. The warmth of the sun failed to let her relax long enough to fall back into a dreamless sleep. She'd never felt so tired in her life, she was sure of it.

Her phone lay charging on the nightstand by her bed, and had vibrated too many times to count in the past while. It buzzed again, oddly closer to her head, or somehow the vibrations had gotten louder and threatened to shake her fully awake. Groaning, she finally reached for it and pulled it close while still under the covers. The screen's brightness nearly blinded her. She could barely open her eyes, but when she did she saw that she'd missed eight calls.

Skylar. *Seriously?*

Her eyes adjusted to the bright light of the screen and caught the time in the corner.

9 a.m.

Oh crap, school!

She jumped out of bed, her brain screaming at her that maybe today, just today, would be a good time to skip school. But the heaviness in her head faded quickly as she frantically ran from her room to the bathroom then back to her room to get dressed.

Ryan's back, she thought as a small smile danced on her lips. *He's going to be at school.*

She raced down the stairs and towards the kitchen with her shoelaces flicking against the wood of the stairs. She had no time to make breakfast; school had started nearly half an hour ago. All she could manage was coffee before heading out the door to walk to school.

Cab it today, Atlanta. It's faster.

She agreed with her inner dialogue and headed around the corner to the main road by her house.

Luckily, she found one the moment she reached the corner of the street, but traffic kept her for another thirty minutes until she finally arrived at Calen High. By then she was already tapping her hands against her knees, wishing the cab could sprout wings and fly. Or she could.

Ten a.m. I can still make next class.

The school stood magnificently with its gothic architecture beaming under the flaming sun. The cement, copper tone gargoyles at the entrance were shimmering as they faced one another. Their wings wrapped around their backs as if to symbolize their dormant powers kept hidden under the static metallic stillness.

Her backpack swung behind her as she ran towards the entrance. She stopped at the frozen gargoyles to tie her shoelace, alternating from one foot to the other under the statue's long shadow. She didn't dare glance up at the beasts, remembering her uncle's story. She shivered at the memory of what the magnificent beasts could do. The thought of fighting them alone made her blood chill.

Getting up, she lifted her head and hesitated a moment, struck by the detail of the beast closest to her. It was cement, but for a moment her eyes saw a spectrum of colors alternating shades. Her gaze formed a bizarre image of the statue that was no longer bronze, but rather she could see its body in dark grey, its veins like bumps in its semi-obscured face. She dismissed the illusion her mind was tricking her with, blaming the lack of sleep for what she was imagining, and hurried up the stairs.

She suddenly staggered and fell to one knee. She felt as if she were—for the briefest of moments—being pulled back to the statue by some force, dragging her back down the steps. Her breath caught and she shook off the feeling. *It's the wind.* She shook her head and huffed, forcing herself to stand and walk back up the steps to the school's entrance. There was no resistance as she walked, no pull to drag her back or stop her. The stupid feeling had just been in her head.

She paused as she reached for the door handle and turned back to glare at the gargoyle. She opened her mouth to mutter something stupid at it, but as she stared a loud call in the air above her cut her off.

There it was. A souvenir from her nightmare had followed her to school.

Stupid raven!

The sight of the bird stalled her and a shiver rippled through her body. It was like the dream had become a sleepless reality, and the reality a sleepless dream. The perplexity of the moment hypnotized her but she broke free, yanking the door to the school open. The school bell rang, signaling the eleven o'clock lunch period.

The cab dropped me off at ten. How did a whole hour fly by?

In confusion, she took out her phone and checked the time. The digital numbers flashed eleven, confirming that an hour had passed in a blink. As if the raven outside had stolen those sixty minutes with one glare from its flaming red eyes. Atlanta headed to her locker, dazed and confused as she marched to it. She hid her face next to the open locker door and struggled to catch her breath.

"Where the hell were you?" a voice came from behind her. Skylar's hand landed on her shoulder and her golden hair swung into view. "I called you, like, a gazillion times."

Atlanta's gasps for air subsided as the soothing familiarity of the sound behind her brought her back to the organized chaos that was high school. She shoved her bag inside the locker and slammed the door, turning to Skylar and trying to bury the debris of her hectic morning behind the brown of her eyes and a forced smile. "I woke up late," Atlanta replied. "Can you believe my alarm snoozed six times and I didn't twitch?"

"What were you up to last night?" Skylar asked, her tone shifting from annoyance to sincere concern.

"I think I've just been worried about...stuff," Atlanta sighed. She and Skylar automatically started walking towards the cafeteria.

They walked through the hallways swayed with whispers, chuckles, and loud laughs that combined to form the everyday cacophony of sound that was the atmosphere of Calen High. By the doors that led to the cafeteria a group of people gathered, and to both girls it seemed like one of those random brawls that broke out nearly every day in school. In the middle of the crowd, his thick black hair flashing while surrounded by his teammates, stood Ryan Toller.

"It's him," Skylar chirped as he elbowed Atlanta. They stopped a couple of feet away from the huddle surrounding Ryan.

Atlanta's silence and gaze fixed on Ryan were the only responses Skylar got. She stood there waiting for Ryan to look her way. The noises of the lockers slamming, the whispered rumors and the laughs hidden behind anxious hearts, faded into silence as they settled in the background of Atlanta's mind. Seconds of waiting felt like years as her heart longed for a glimpse of his green eyes.

Skylar was tapping her on the shoulder, whispering and chuckling. "Not interested, eh?" She giggled. "Really?"

Ryan's deep green eyes flashed their way, and Atlanta froze. He high-fived his teammates and threw smiles around like a tree graciously spreading its leaves on a windy autumn day. He strolled their way, his whole body studied and memorized by Atlanta...and apparently Skylar, too.

Atlanta's heart went racing, and the muscles in her cheeks stretched robotically as his eyes met hers. She wanted to race over and hug him.

She tried to fight the paralysis that her nerves dictated upon her, but she couldn't. All she could do was grin at him like a loon.

Ryan dropped his backpack and made his way towards them. His pace quickened, and he almost ran the remaining distance between them. He wrapped his arms around Skylar's waist, hugging her tight and lifting her off the floor, laying a soft and quick kiss on her shivering lips. Skylar seemed to freeze, and when he dropped her back on her feet she was staring at nothing in particular, obviously shocked. She began to quickly blush, and it was all Atlanta could do not to laugh out loud.

Then Ryan turned to Atlanta and gave her a brief hug, looked at her shocked and perplexed eyes, and smiled briefly. "Hey, Atlanta," he said, keeping his tone distinctly polite. "Haven't seen you in a while." Then looked back at Skylar and grinned.

Atlanta tried to say something, but nothing came to mind. Silence paraded her brain. *Nothing? Seriously, you can't think of anything to say? You haven't seen him in forever! You thought he was dead! Can't you manage something? Anything? Wait. He's not even really looking at me. What's up? Did something happen? Did he get hurt?* She gazed down and he looked perfectly fine. Handsome as—*Stop it! Focus, Atlanta!* She fought the paralyzed tip of her tongue, and through the conflicted emotions she was feeling she finally managed to utter a couple of words. "I'm fine," she said, her voice quivering. "Glad you're back." She turned to Skylar, ready to make a fast getaway and found her friend still lost in the midst of blushes and smiles. She blinked in confusion, turning back to Ryan. Everything felt off again. Maybe it was hormones? Or being a teenager, but crap!

Except, something was different. The way he looked at her was different. His deep green eyes didn't feel like the tunnel of evergreen she liked gazing into every day. Rather, in the peculiarity of this moment they felt like a dark well with a 'No Trespassing' sign hanging over it.

What made things even worse was that it felt like Ryan didn't even register she was there. There was an indifference towards her, a forgetting of the river of feelings that had seemed to flow both ways just a month before. And worse, the course of that river seemed to have changed direction towards her closest and only friend.

Atlanta dropped the book she had in her hands and quickly began walking past them. "I gotta go."

"Where are you going?" Skylar called out, clearly confused.

"Bathroom," Atlanta whispered as a tear rolled down her cheek.

He didn't even notice the tear, she thought as her mind spun on overdrive. She ran faster towards the bathrooms, nearly staggering, her whole emotional being scattered in the array of broken thoughts her heart had created. She didn't know whether to feel betrayed or happy for Skylar. After all, her friend had always been drooling over Ryan.

But now wasn't the time to figure out how she felt. She needed to know where the debris of her emotions fell so she could curl up right next to it. She wanted to go back home. She tried not to think about Ryan and Skylar standing at the cafeteria, but she couldn't erase the image. She groaned as she realized she'd dropped her book. It probably rested on the ground between Ryan and Skylar's feet, its title flashing in bright white, *The Idiot* by Dostoevsky.

That was exactly how Atlanta felt.

THE DAYS AND NIGHTS that followed Ryan's return to Calen High passed like centuries through Atlanta's stormy mind. She spent most of her time in the basement where the sandbags and rubber walls suffered the thundering pounding of her fists. She grunted and panted, cried and screamed. She would curl up on the couch in the basement and drown her mind in melancholic drama, then drift off into a sleepless slumber and invite the nightmares in. When she woke up in the morning, she'd dismiss the dark dreams in between angry punches and kicks.

Skylar's calls were relentless, but Atlanta rarely answered. When she did, she used excuses like being busy with reading, homework, or sleeping the days away just so she wouldn't have to see her friend. It was painful to go out with Skylar, because she never was alone. She and Ryan were suddenly dating, and Atlanta felt like she was being left behind, broken and dismissed.

Idiot! She admonished herself for not expressing her feelings out loud to either Skylar or Ryan. *It wouldn't have made a difference,* she thought to herself. If she'd told Skylar about the nature of Calen's underground reality, she could have never gotten closer to Ryan. She criticized her anxious nature, her paralyzed tongue when he'd hypnotized her with smiles. She tried to recall every moment they shared, every little breath they both rhythmically exhaled at the same moment, as if to signal their unprecedented bond and connection. She looked for mistakes she might've made, thoughts she didn't share, and signals she had failed to pick up on, but it all seemed surreal. He never noticed. She could have sworn there'd been an undercurrent between the two of them. Sure, she hadn't admitted she liked him out loud, but neither had he. Yet...hadn't there kind of been something there?

She sighed. Whatever. She'd denied her own feelings and he'd never noticed. It didn't exist. It never had.

She sighed again and kicked another sandbag. It broke open and sand exploded from the rip and rained down on her.

Ryan's return to Calen was surreal.

It's like he's somebody else completely. She stomped over to the punching bag, ignoring the sand still falling. She stood glaring at the bag, her eyes burning, fists clenched. She drew images of Ryan in her mind, and immediately began throwing punches, sand flying off her shoulders and out of her hair. She fought against the bag as if it were a nemesis she needed to defeat. She was only inches away from grabbing one of her knives and ripping the leather bag to shreds, when a coughing brought her out of her angry trance.

James was standing at the bottom of the stairs, watching her, his eyes narrowed as if he were trying to understand what was happening. "I think if you really want," he said, "we can set a flame thrower at it and get this over with."

Atlanta puffed and blew strands of her hair out of her face. Her chest heaved with bottled up aggression and the desire to go back to punishing the bag. She waited patiently for her uncle to say what he had come to say.

"You know, if I had known it would come to this one day I would've bought more and stored them aside," he joked. He glanced over that the emptied sandbag. "Maybe some water so we could make a beach, too?"

Great, everyone's a comedian now! Atlanta threw an aimless punch at the bag. "Just practicing."

James forced a tight smile. "I'd offer to do a little one-on-one, but I have a feeling I might have a few broken bones by the time we're done."

"I haven't beaten you once," Atlanta snapped.

"You haven't been this angry, either," James pointed out. "Want to talk about it?"

"Nope." Atlanta shook her head and nailed the bag few more times.

"Is this about Ryan?" When she didn't answer, he nodded. "I heard he's been acting a little...differently. He's dating Skylar, right?"

"They're a perfect match," Atlanta replied, trying not to sound as if it bothered her. "I'm—" punch, "happy—" punch, "for them." Punch-punch.

James studied her a second. "I guess you're right," he said slowly. "Do you think it's serious?"

"Does it matter?" she snapped, turning to glare at him.

"In more ways than one," James replied, not meeting her gaze. Then he straightened his shoulders. "But we'll leave that for another day. I actually came down here for a different reason."

Atlanta began unzipping her gloves and grabbed her water bottle. "What?" She knew she was being bitchy, but couldn't stop herself. She was relieved that her uncle wasn't pressing the Ryan and Skylar sitting in a tree issue.

"Marcus called a meeting at the Dome." He turned to head back up the stairs. "Everyone's going to be there. Ryan included."

"Great." Atlanta sniffed and tossed her gloves to a side. "Have fun, I guess."

"You're coming."

Atlanta shook her head. "No."

James sighed and headed down the stairs again. He crossed the distance between them in two quick strides. He held her hands in his and waited to speak until she looked him in the eye. "Whatever you're going through, take a breath. All that emotional turmoil...it sucks. I know it does. I can only imagine how it feels seeing Ryan and Skylar together."

"I don't know what you're talking about," Atlanta replied, holding back tears.

James smiled tenderly. "I may be a klutz and a bad cook, but I'm not stupid." He wiped her cheek. "But you know what? Hide it all you want, that's fine. I won't push. But use that rush of emotion wisely. Concentrate. Build on it. Don't let it destroy you."

"It's fine." She pulled away from him and ran a hand through her hair. "I'm fine."

"Sure you are," James mocked. "You've been to every meeting since Colin's death, and you've been at the forefront of the search for Ryan. And now that he's back, now that you have a chance to really talk to him on home turf, you don't want to go?"

"Uncle James, please."

James held a hand up to stop her. "This meeting is because of you," he said. "You're the reason everyone's at the Dome right now, waiting for us. Whether you like it or not, this is not a meeting you can miss."

What do they want from me? Atlanta looked at James in confusion, her thoughts on Ryan suddenly benched in light of this recent turn in events. She swallowed and nodded once at her uncle. Suddenly, everything that had been happening around them felt like it was about to get real. Very real.

James turned to head back upstairs. "Ten minutes, Atlanta," he called over his shoulder.

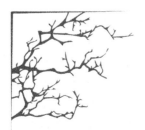

Chapter 19

HER UNCLE INSISTED she suit up for the meeting. The odd request had her biting her tongue in curiosity. And worry. This was just a meeting and she rarely needed to be prepared for a fight when heading for the Dome. The last time she had, Ryan had almost torn them apart while compelled.

Great. What's going to happen this time?

They took the tunnels and drove in verbal silence, each lost in their own thoughts. The only sound was the revving of their bikes echoing through the passageways. When they arrived at the Dome, two guards stood waiting for them. Marcus had stationed them to escort them. Already Atlanta was itching to reach for her weapons. The situation appeared less and less the meeting kind of calling. They followed the guards; again, no words were spoken between her and James. She glanced at him several times as they headed to the assembly hall, but his gazed remained straight ahead. Everything about his posture and gait told her something was going on. *What aren't you telling me?*

Inside the hall, everyone appeared to be there already. No one was saying a word. Dead silence. All heads turned in their direction when they entered. Like her uncle, Atlanta kept her gaze fixed forward, trying to avoid eye contact with Ryan, who was now staring at her with such intensity it frightened her.

Past the shadowy corners of the Dome, inside the structure that was externally ornamented with the same cement monsters as those at Calen High, Atlanta stood in her crimson suit next to her uncle at one end of the long table. Across from them sat Marcus, his fingers intertwined, his dark brown eyes gazing at them. His breath was unnoticeable in the silence of the Dome. All that could be heard was the soft beating of the hearts of the Druids, and the impatient tapping of feet on the ground from Ryan and the Wolves who had accompanied him.

"There's been an intolerable disturbance in the peace we've maintained for over a century," Marcus stated as he softly slammed his hands on the table, the heaviness of his utterance drawing all eyes and ears towards him. "Most of you are clueless to what has been lurking in the shadows and murdering our own. Louis first, and now Colin. A murder in each family, so as to force us to engage in a skirmish." His eyes fell on Ryan's and he stared into them for a moment, closely observing the reaction of the new head of the wolf pack.

Atlanta followed Marcus' gaze and gave herself a moment to look at her once-close friend. It seemed weird to think they weren't close anymore. But, somehow, a wall had been built between them and she had no idea how to tear it down. She squinted as she took a closer look at him. *He's different. It's not me. It's him. He's even starting to look different.* He'd changed. Matured, maybe. Angry, probably. He'd lost his dad and was now the head of his pack. That would force someone to change. *Maybe I should have tried talking to him. Maybe it's too late.*

"This morning, regretfully, two of our own had to be... they had to be... they're gone. They were scheming to attack your kind," Marcus finished in a consistent and strong tone, addressing Ryan directly. Marcus then turned toward James. They seemed to be sharing a thought, and then James nodded.

Marcus turned to face Atlanta, and a quick shudder raced through her before she quickly regained her composure.

James inhaled deeply and glanced around at all those around the table. "About a century ago, hybrids—a combination of vampires and witches—were created by a sadistic witch named Adelaide," James said in a voice that rose as he moved his head from right to left, aiming his speech at everyone in the room. "These hybrids have powers beyond measure. They're capable of turning Calen to dust if they're allowed to roam freely. We stopped them with the help of another witch. Beatrice helped the Druids lock them away during what you all know as the Insurgence. The door that's right under our feet is the only barrier between them and us. It has remained locked ever since." He paused, waiting for the murmuring of those around him to stop. "However, Adelaide escaped before the Druids could get to her. She was known to have kept one of her hybrids by her side at all times. Now the only explanation for the murders and the compulsion of the head of the Werewolf pack is that Adelaide's hybrid is in Calen. It wouldn't be farfetched to say that Adelaide might be here as well."

Ryan snorted, and then let out a mocking laugh that echoed in the room.

Marcus glared at him, anger oozing from his eyes.

Ryan's expression turned from mockery and laughter into disgust and indignation. "Did you make up a story to mask what the vampires did to my father?" Ryan growled.

Marcus snarled and slammed his fists onto the table. "You're a fool!" he shouted. "Have you not learned to keep your atrocious thoughts inside your small mind until they clear?"

"Enough!" James grunted. He turned to look at Ryan. "Your accusations are the reason this meeting is being held. Many truths need to be told and you, young man, will listen until there is no more to say."

Ryan's claws stretched from his fingers, his eyes glowing yellow. He clenched his fists, then turned his eyes from Marcus to James and fell silent. "Fine. Say whatever you have to say, and then we're gone."

James sighed and took a long breath, letting it exhales as he set his shoulders. "We *all* need to maintain our unity if we want to maintain the peace. The hybrid can compel a Werewolf." James glanced meaningfully at the new wolfpack leader. "Hence what happened to Ryan in the Dome a few weeks back. Its powers can extend to vampires, yet not their elders." James ignored Ryan's exaggerated snort. "Druids cannot be controlled by the hybrid. Neither can the hybrids enter the premises of their homes." He'd begun walking around the table, gesturing with his hands as he spoke. "What Adelaide wants is to open the door and free her army of hybrids. If that happens, our city will burn." From the corner of her eye, Atlanta could see her uncle turn to her. "That door can only be opened by Atlanta."

Atlanta didn't know whether to be afraid or confident. Her fear compelled her into believing that the vampires or werewolves would attempt to kill her if it meant preventing the opening of the door. But she was reassured by Marcus before it became a rational fear. If she were to be killed, that wouldn't ensure the door would remain closed. It would only mean that the power to open the door would be passed on to another witch, one they wouldn't know. So, she was far from being in danger. In fact, according to her uncle and Marcus, she would be protected by all means possible.

Her confidence came from the knowledge that she held the key to saving the city from going through another insurgence. Her thoughts inspired her to believe she could be the one to eradicate the hybrid. She just needed to see its face. Thoughts flicked through her mind at a ridiculous rate. With each nightmare that roared through her sleep, carrying its camouflaged, dark, and shadowy face, the hybrid's features got clearer. *I just have to stay alive long enough to find it and destroy it.*

She felt the eyes of every person, vampire, and Werewolf in the assembly hall staring at her. She could feel their concern, their worry, their anger and, worst of all, their fear. They began talking in low voices. She listened quietly as plans were made to keep her safe, all while stealing glances at Ryan as he watched her from where he sat. She tried to read his features, to understand what was going behind those cold eyes of his, but she failed. *It doesn't matter anymore. Focus, Atlanta. Stay alive. Find the hybrid. Or Adelaide. Whatever it takes to stop anyone from coming to open the door. Focus. Just focus.*

But she couldn't. The longer she stood there, the center of attention, the harder it was for her to push away the thoughts racing through her mind. The fate of Calen rested on her shoulders. What if she screwed up? What if she opened the door by accident? What if she let her city die?

The last thought scared the hell out of her.

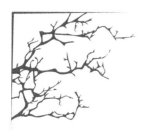

Chapter 20

NIGHTS DRAGGED BY AS every creature in Calen held its breath, waiting for imminent disaster to strike. Yet, for nearly a week, the city seemed to be at peace. The neon lights flashed their cold white as the night burned into day and the day melted into night again.

Atlanta spent her days and nights training, pushing herself to the limit, using the pain and heartache she felt as a motivator to push her forward. Since the meeting at the Dome she hadn't seen Ryan, and made it a point to avoid him as much as possible at school. She avoided school as much as possible, but she couldn't avoid it forever. And James made her go. She would be safe there, and it was a good distraction.

Even though Atlanta's fierce wall of emotion towered higher than Calen's skyscrapers, Skylar found a way back into Atlanta's daily routine. The persistence of a best friend was met with the blunt dodging and escaping that Atlanta relentlessly drew on, yet seeing each other in school nearly every day made it something of a must for the two of them to talk.

And those days at school only gave Atlanta more images to place at the receiving end of her punches that thundered against the sandbags. Skylar and Ryan holding hands, whispering to each other, melting into one another in every corridor of the school. Atlanta was forced to find a different route to class whenever spotted them.

That wasn't the only change that rocked Atlanta at school.

A new principal had been appointed, and although no one cared where this man came from, Atlanta had to pretend to be just as oblivious. Seeing Marcus every day wasn't something she was accustomed to, and she was honestly against him becoming the head of the school. It was awkward. And stupid. Her uncle told her it was to keep an even closer watch on what happened in the school, but Atlanta knew it was more of an attempt to keep an eye on her. *It was safe.* Hadn't those been James' words? Safe, and a distraction? *Bloody hell.*

It was torture.

So, she waited for disaster to strike. Knowing it could happen at any moment. She watched the skies for the stupid raven, watched her nightmares for a closer look at the beast hiding inside. Watched the roads for cars coming after her, crouched by bushes, sprinted around corners, carried her weapon. And yet the days slowly passed.

Then one of the gargoyle statues around Calen High vanished. Everyone at school laughed and wondered if a competing high school had stolen it.

Except she knew.

It was the only sign that the hybrid wasn't far away, lurking in shadows around them, waiting for the right moment.

Atlanta slammed her fists against the sandbag in front of her, her breaths measured, her heartbeat steady. She usually stayed in the basement if she wasn't at school, and James was always around. The more time she spent training, the greater her confidence in her skills grew. She barely heard the doorbell upstairs.

Her crimson red suit stretched on her skin and its velvet smoothness shone in the fluorescent lights that beamed above her head. She stopped training when she heard her uncle's heavy footsteps make their way across the hall and to the door. She glanced at the clock behind her and frowned. It was nearly midnight. *Who could possibly be here this time of night? Has something happened?*

She heard her uncle opening the door, and her breath caught when Ryan's voice echoed in the house.

"I'm sorry to be coming by this late, but is Skylar here?"

Skylar?

"No, she isn't here," James replied. "I actually haven't seen in her in some time. She and Atlanta don't hang out as often as they used to. Is something wrong?"

"I'm not sure," Ryan replied. Atlanta moved toward the staircase as she listened to the conversation. Ryan cleared his throat. "She hasn't replied to my texts or calls. I went up to her place and she wasn't there. Michael said she never came home from school."

Atlanta sighed and made her way upstairs. An air of uneasiness took over at the sight of Ryan by the door. She paused for a moment, meeting his eyes, then walked towards him. "Is everything okay?"

"I can't find Skylar." Ryan looked genuinely worried.

"You lost her already?" she asked sarcastically.

James shot her a look that she couldn't miss even if she'd closed her eyes.

"Sorry." She tried again, her tone taking on a more concerned note, "Did you walk her home from school?"

"No," he replied. "Last I saw her was when she was getting in her car at the end of the day."

"Did you check around the house? In the gardens? The willow tree?"

"I did. Her car isn't anywhere around the house, or the neighborhood."

It's a trap! The words echoed in her head with such urgency, it made her sway. It was as if a small warning sign had been lit up inside her, flashing with such intensity that it was all she could think of.

She didn't know why she'd never considered that, if the hybrid was trying to get to her, he would probably go after the people closest to her. The idea was one she had read in countless books and seen implemented in tons of movies. If that was what the hybrid was going for, then she knew this was one trap she was going to fall into head first without even questioning her own safety. Two could play at that game. "We can't stay here," she declared suddenly. "We have to be out there looking for her. Let's start with her car. If we find Skylar's car, we find her."

She glanced at her uncle, and almost flinched at the way he was looking at her. She could only imagine the conflict he was wrestling with. On the one hand, their duty was to protect, and it seemed Skylar needed their help. On the other hand, Atlanta needed to be protected, too.

And her uncle wasn't stupid; she knew that well. It was clear he felt the same way she did about this whole thing.

James finally nodded and opened the door wider for Ryan to come in. The three of them raced downstairs. James opened the secret passage to the training area, and they bolted downwards to where the bikes were parked. Before Atlanta could suggest anything, James tossed Ryan a helmet and said, "You're riding with me."

Atlanta sighed in relief. With the way she needed to keep her head clear, having Ryan's arms wrapped around her waist for the remainder of the night would not help.

She looked at James and he winked before his face disappeared behind his helmet's mask. *I owe you one.*

The roar of the engines echoed through the passageways. James and Ryan shot forward, and Atlanta followed closely behind. The fluorescent lights of the basement receded, and the city's mixture of red, blue, and green neon lights flickered into view ahead of them.

They started out by cruising the suburbs of Calen, from house to house and garden to garden, but there was no sign of Skylar anywhere. James suggested they pay her house another visit before they ventured into the city's downtown area, but she wasn't there. The lights of the house were out and, strangely enough, even Michael wasn't home.

That doesn't make things any better, Atlanta thought as she gazed at the dark windows.

The midnight silence made the doubts and concerns ring loud in her head as the rest of the city slept to the roars of their bikes. The lights from the offices in the skyscrapers began to flicker out one by one as the search continued. They passed by Calen High to see if she had even left the school to begin with; the car wasn't there, and the sight of the absent gargoyle reminded Atlanta what they were up against.

They stopped at a small diner where Ryan swore he'd spotted Skylar sitting alone at a table. Atlanta watched Ryan race towards the glass window, his claws pulling out slightly in his excitement.

"Ryan, wait!" she called after him.

But he was already at the diner. A patron jumped back at the sight of Ryan's hands on the glass window. She fumbled out of the booth and raced towards the back, where Atlanta was sure she'd be screaming at the cook about a wolf at the window.

Ryan turned and raced back to Atlanta and James.

"It's not her," he said in frustration.

"Really?" Atlanta snapped. "What the hell were you thinking?"

Ryan's head snapped at her, and she could see the familiar yellow glow in his eyes.

No wonder the girl ran away when she saw that.

"I was thinking that my *girlfriend* might be safe, not in the hands of some hybrid."

"Next time, either Atlanta or I will check," James said. "We don't want any Werewolf stories being passed around."

Ryan frowned and glared at them.

"Where do we go now?" Atlanta asked. "It's nearly three in the morning and we've looked everywhere."

"We're not giving up because you're tired," Ryan grunted.

"Who said anything about giving up? Or being tired?" Atlanta snapped defensively. *She's my friend, too, you know? Before you two started sharing saliva!*

"Not the time for arguing," James interfered in a calm, judge-like manner. "Enough, you two. Whatever your issues are with each other, drop it. We need to find Skylar."

It took a moment, but Atlanta finally caved in and agreed. "You're right. Sorry, Uncle James."

Ryan sighed. "Yeah, let's find Skylar."

The two sat silent on the bikes while Ryan paced on the sidewalk beside them.

"Where does Skylar hang out?" James asked.

"My house." Atlanta and Ryan said at the same time. "Or by the tree at her house. She's slept outside a couple times." She glanced at Ryan, waiting to see if he'd say something she didn't want to hear. Luckily, he just kept pacing. Suddenly a thought hit her and she felt her eyes widen. "Remember the three towers that look out on the lake?" she asked Ryan.

"Yes, the old Matlyn Co. factory. What about them?"

"Skylar used to go up there after school when she wasn't feeling good. I went with her a couple of times. She never went there at night, but it's worth a try."

"It's worth a shot," James said as he turned the engine back on. "We've been everywhere else." He looked to Ryan. "Hop on."

"Nah, I can run there." Ryan turned, about to start sprinting.

"I know you can," James said sternly. "Hop on."

The look in his eyes frightened Atlanta. Her uncle was never this serious. What bothered her even more was how Ryan gazed back challengingly.

"You'll only slow me down." Ryan crossed his arms over his chest, ready to argue.

"We need to be prepared," James said. "If something's wrong you'll be needing your strength. Don't waste that running."

Ryan hesitated for a moment, then sighed and got on the back of James' bike. Atlanta put on her helmet and followed them as they drove away. She kept her eyes locked on Ryan's back as her mind swam.

He's not himself. Hasn't been since he got back. Something doesn't feel right.

The towers were almost perfect cylinders with their dark-blue glass walls blazing under the purple sky. There were small red lights that flickered on the roofs. The three buildings were not so far apart, one in front of the other two to form a triangle. Skylar's car was parked by one of them, almost hidden in between several other cars that were there.

"We'll cover more ground if we split up," Ryan said. "One of us for each tower."

Atlanta looked at her uncle. James looked like he wanted to argue but, realizing the danger, he relented. "Okay."

"Fine, let's go," Ryan said, and bolted forwards.

Atlanta turned to head toward the second tower when her uncle grabbed her arm.

"Careful," he said, his eyes fixed on Ryan in the distance.

"I know," Atlanta assured him.

"No," James said, shaking his head slowly. "You really don't." He looked at her seriously. "Promise me you won't do anything stupid."

"I'm a witch living among Druids, werewolves, and vampires, being hunted by some hybrid monstrosity," Atlanta replied. "You're going to have to define *stupid*."

James shook his head and smiled, then began running in the opposite direction.

The three of them headed in separate ways, each bolting towards the roof of one of the three buildings.

Oddly, even though she knew she was heading into a trap, she could not have felt more confident. She thought she'd prepared herself for whatever creature was waiting for her. Atlanta knew if Skylar was up there, she only had to get her away from him.

Then I'm really going to make that thing suffer! It wants me? Well, it's not taking me down without a fight. Get Skylar out, and if I can't kill the beast, die before I let the door open.

The main gate of the building slid sideways as it opened. The place was empty; she could hear the echo of her footsteps. The marathon of thoughts in her head was silenced by her composed confidence as she forced herself to expect a sudden attack at any second. The building was nearly twenty stories high, so the stairs weren't much of an option. The elevator, on the other hand, was waiting for her, its grey metal door opening before she even had the chance to press the button. She stepped inside, knowing that every move she would make from now on had been previously orchestrated for her, perfectly set.

But she knew she was one step ahead of the hybrid.

She had seen it coming, she knew the trap.

For a brief second, she wondered if it was intelligence or plain stupidity. She shook the thought away, realizing that the only advantage knowing this was a trap gave her reflexes a split second to react faster, her thoughts would not be scattered while she fought. She wouldn't be shocked. The adrenaline would be controlled, directed, and mastered.

The elevator dinged.

Atlanta looked up as the number twenty flickered in digital black on the blue screen. The doors slid open.

The lights on this floor were on, and to the side she saw a white door with a wide metal handle. Above the door was a green fluorescent sign that signaled the emergency exit. She opened the door and found the narrow staircase that led to the roof.

She remembered the place; Skylar had dragged her up there to show her the lake and the city from above. This time, however, she had a feeling she'd be seeing a much less pleasant scene.

She climbed the stairs and held her breath as she reached the final door. She exhaled slowly and pushed the door open, prepared for anything. The sound of the wind softly bombarded the air coming out the vents. The roof's floor was filled with pebbles that she could hear being forced into one another as she walked over them.

"Skylar," she called out. She heard an adjacent sound of moving pebbles across from her. There was no reply.

She took careful steps forward and slid her blade from its sheath on her back. Her fingers curled around the hilt, holding it tight. She followed the sound of the pebbles cracking, making sure she made as little noise as possible.

When she slid around a large vent to the other side of it, she froze.

He stood a few yards away, his left side towards her. He was wearing a grey coat that fluttered about in the wind. He stood next to the flashing red light, his hood pulled over his head. He seemed to be staring out at the lake, lost in its serenity.

Got you! She approached him with the blade in her hand. She knew his movements had to be swift, especially if he could take Louis and Colin. She focused her eyes on his legs, waiting for a leap. He moved his head towards her, his face shadowed by the hood.

Her heart raced and her grip on the blade tightened. He walked towards her, slowly and confidently, his face downward.

He lifted the hood off his head.

Atlanta felt her heart stop. "Michael?"

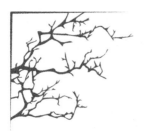

Chapter 21

ATLANTA STOOD IN PARALYZED astonishment. *Michael?*

For what felt like an eternity a dreary silence would hover by, then the wind would continue its slight hammering. The light of the moon was a brilliant white that overcast the dim, glowing stars. Atlanta felt a sudden shiver race through her, her senses scattered, her confidence shattered. Nothing could have prepared her for this.

Over the many years of friendship with Skylar, she hadn't interacted much with Michael. He kept mostly to himself. He never missed a day at school, and even there his voice was barely heard. He blended in, almost into the shadows. He was one of those kids who was excessively silent. She had always traced that silence back to the feelings of abandonment he must have experienced when his parents left.

His skin was a pale white, his hair a dark shade of brown slightly darker than the color of his eyes. His shoulders were broad, which was unlikely for his young age. She knew that he was always the highest achiever in his grade growing up, and even when he and Skylar were left to fend for themselves the grades on his transcript didn't change the smallest bit.

There had always been a peculiarity in his behavior, but Atlanta always related it to the lack of parental guidance in his life. However, he seemed to be the one who knew where to find Skylar before they did.

Or not? Is he here for another reason?

Atlanta fought back the doubts her mind was throwing at her. Michael was just a boy. There was no way he could be anything else. Surely, they would have seen that before.

He was leaning onto the ledge of the roof as Atlanta approached him. He was looking straight down, and then he turned around to face her. When his face appeared in the moonlight, Atlanta half expected to see the face of the hybrid there instead, the lurking visage from her nightmares. But it was Michael. His face was pale and he looked swallowed in a state of distress. He was speechless for a while as he stood paralyzed and stared at Atlanta with wide eyes.

"Michael?" Atlanta's tone was not as strong as she had hoped it would sound. "Where did Skylar go?"

His voice was thin and shaky; the words were rising from beneath a turbulent heart. He was trying to say something, but his tongue was tied in a weird kind of hesitance and shock.

Atlanta sheathed her blade. "Michael, can you hear me?"

Michael turned away from Atlanta and walked back to where he had previously stood. He looked down from the roof and then back at her. It felt as if he had been forced into silence by something that was on the ground.

Atlanta hurried toward the ledge, her heart skipping a beat, scared of what she might see. The pebbles echoed her footsteps as the night was beginning to fall into dawn. She stood right next to Michael, the wind howling and roaring, his coat slamming against her body. She put her hand on the stone ledge and looked down. She searched for whatever was scaring Michael, but couldn't identify a single thing that was out of the ordinary.

A circular cobblestone floor occupied the space between the three buildings, with a bench parallel to each. Further behind that area was a metal fence that was missing pieces in many areas. The forest behind it was darkened, and the lake was moon-lit. When the wind would cease, the sound of the crickets would rhythmically echo.

She gazed at the lake for a moment and back at the area in between the buildings, but there was nothing to be seen.

"What is it?" she asked, shaking her head in bewilderment.

He looked at her and uttered an incoherent word. When she frowned at him in confusion, he breathed in and leaned his head down again. Then he pointed with his fingers at the benches underneath.

"S-She j-jumped," he said in a shaking voice. "I saw her jump."

Atlanta's heart jumped into her throat, and she held back a startled gasp. Her nervousness drove itself into the pit of her stomach then rose again. Her eyes widened and she hurriedly and frantically searched where Michael's finger was pointing to, but she could barely make out anything.

The area below was well lit, with three posts beaming white light. Even though she was on the roof of the twentieth floor, every detail underneath was apparent. If there was something odd down there, she should have been able to see it.

Suddenly all thoughts of the hybrid disappeared, her readiness for a fight dispersing at the thought of Skylar jumping. She thought that it wouldn't be far from Michael to hallucinate what he said he saw, it wasn't far from him to think he saw his sister jumping; it was Michael after all. The kid who once swore to his sister that he talked to the willow tree by their house. He was the kid who had an imaginary friend up until he was in seventh grade. He wasn't an ordinary boy. But that would have been better to believe at that moment than the thought of her best friend jumping.

She didn't. He's imagining it.

Then why is her car here?

Atlanta quickly looked at the roofs of the other two buildings, but couldn't see anything. She couldn't know if Skylar was on either one of them, or if Ryan or James had found her. She turned back to Michael and held his arms.

"Michael, are you sure you saw Skylar jump?" she asked, her voice trembling as tears began to roll down her cheeks.

Michael gazed back at her, stupefied. It was almost as if he didn't understand her, like she was speaking a foreign language far from his comprehension. His body was shivering and his arms were curling onto his body as if to escape her touch. He stepped backwards, then took several more. He was blindly heading towards the ledge. He stopped and put his hood back on.

Atlanta knew that, whatever had happened, she had to find out for herself. She had to go back downstairs.

"Wait here," she said assertively.

You can't leave him here. Not like this.

"Maybe, come with me," she whispered, and held her hand out to him.

A sudden thundering sound came from the roof of one of the other buildings. It was a quivering echo of something that was slammed hard against the stone, followed by the sound of rocks breaking and falling.

Michael immediately stepped forward and away from the ledge at the sound. Atlanta dashed towards the side of the roof that was closer to the other building. She couldn't see anything.

The sound thundered through the night sky again, and this time it was accompanied by a deep growl.

"It's Ryan," she whispered to herself.

Atlanta quickly turned to Michael. "Come on, we have to get out of here."

But Michael didn't move.

A peculiar grin took over his face, and his features began to darken grimly. He walked towards the ledge and picked something up. Atlanta immediately recognized the patterned sneakers.

They were Skylar's

Michael turned to her, his grin widening, and then propelled the sneakers through the air. Atlanta followed the trajectory, and as she watched the world around her shifted.

The darkness around her intensified, almost as if the night were trying to take over every ounce of light that existed. It rested heavy on her shoulders, and with it came a sharp pain in her chest that brought her to her knees. It was almost like a stabbing that made her struggle to breathe.

What's happening?

Croaks of ravens echoed, and when she looked up dozens began to appear by the red light next to Michael. Flashes from her nightmares followed and made her scream. It was almost like every single haunting image was a piece of a melancholic puzzle that was being pushed together before her eyes. And that one last piece of that puzzle, the one that had been taunting her all these nights, was not going to come to her sleeping, subconscious mind, but was going to be revealed in the very moment she was in.

Flashes of green light burst through the sky.

Uncle James!

She wanted to call out to him. She wanted him to come and save her from the evil that she felt crawling into her veins. She could feel her veins bursting from the inside, her nerves pumping the darkest of emotions and bleeding into her mind flashes of glaring red eyes.

The ravens ascended and swirled around the moon in circles. They paraded the night sky and their flaming red eyes dripped green rain that burned the pebbles on the floor.

Her knees were trembling and her head fell to the ground as she struggled to hear a stillness in her thoughts, fought to grasp onto a single image that wasn't blurry. Her eyelashes were closing onto one another and she fought to keep them open. She was blacking out. She lifted herself to her knees and felt the ravens a tiny distance away from her head, swirling around her as if casting a spell of everlasting agony over her body. Pain burst through her, touching every inch of her body, leaving no part of her at peace.

In between the vagueness she thought she saw Skylar's face next to the red light, but there was no way to be sure. She couldn't even be sure if the moment she was in was a dark and grim reality, or just a shadow of another nightmare.

Ryan never came to the house. Skylar isn't missing. This is all a nightmare. I'm dreaming, and I'm going to wake up now. Any minute now. Now!

But she didn't. The nightmare had managed to set its claws deep into her senses and nearly dragged every bit of sanity out of her.

The wind howled but could not mask her screams as they pierced the night. She tried to stand up. She placed her hands on the pebbles and squeezed hard, but she was only barely touching them with the tips of her fingers. The muscles of her fingers were numb. She gathered all her strength and pushed herself up on one knee, but the wind pushed her back down.

She looked at the blood on her hands, but it wasn't the usual red she expected to see.

It's green. I'm bleeding green.

She looked past the blur, her eyes sharpening as she took in the one image that had always failed to appear in her nightmares.

Skylar was standing on the ledge, her hair flickering behind her brother's broad figure. The ravens cast a growing shadow behind Skylar's shoulders. Another round of croaks whistled and, far behind them, a slow- burning sun was beginning to rise from behind the forest.

She's alive! She didn't jump!

Atlanta tried to speak. A tiny fragment of her heart was trying to sigh in relief of finding Skylar, but she couldn't even understand what was happening to her own body. She was being torn from the inside out and every muscle inside her was relaxing and contracting involuntarily.

And suddenly, as if someone had flipped a light switch inside her head, everything made perfect sense.

She saw Skylar clearly now, the ravens all around her, her deep green eyes glowing greener in the morning light. She was smiling at Atlanta, a sinister smile that quickly turned into manic laughter.

No! It can't be!

Michael stood completely still in front of his sister, and through the shadows of his hood his true form was beginning to unravel. The malice that was the root of his silence. The disheartened truth behind his never-present smile began to reveal itself in the fangs that protruded from his jaw.

He began moving towards Atlanta, his eyes blazing red.

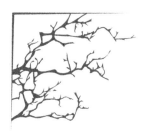

Chapter 22

IN ATLANTA'S MIND SKYLAR'S very name was breaking down, its letters cracking and falling into a pit of a lie that she so much lived rather than just believed. It was more convenient to call Skylar not with the name that she had adopted in that decade, but rather by the name that she was known for.

Adelaide.

The witch let out a malevolent laugh. Adelaide was surrounded by a green mist as the ravens engulfed the perimeter of the roof. Her forest-green eyes were fixed on Atlanta, paralyzed on the ground in agony.

"Did you come to save me, dear friend?" Adelaide whispered as she bent down and brought her face closer to Atlanta's.

She laughed as she slid her long nails down Atlanta's hair and moved them around her face. Atlanta struggled to control the movement of her body, but she failed miserably. She was feeling her legs move involuntarily, as if she were compelled.

I thought Druids couldn't be compelled. How is this possible?

A shiver raced through her. She had begun to completely understand the gravity of her situation. Of every time that she thought she was hiding the nature of her life from her best friend to protect her.

It was all a trick. It was all a game. From the very beginning. They've been planning this for years.

She couldn't help but think back to every day that led to this final, dark moment. Skylar has been her friend forever, and the fact that she was Adelaide all this time made Atlanta doubt her own sanity.

What else have I been blind to? What else did I miss?

Years of training and late-night missions all boiled down to one thought in her head: She was not prepared. She knew nothing of the world around her, and for all these years had lived under the illusion of control. She had been played from the get-go, pushed right and left until this final moment, lying on the ground in front of the one person who meant her the most harm.

Atlanta tried to move, but it was pointless. Whatever sort of compulsion she was under it had a complete hold over her, and try as she might she couldn't break free of its spell.

In the distance, the growls grew louder. She tried to turn her head towards them, but it was like she had been frozen in place. There was a sound of hovering like that of an approaching airplane, and she could feel the winds bend to whatever force was arriving.

From the corner of her eye a green light burst in bright glory, crashing into the pebbles on the roof. Two bodies slammed onto the ground, hovered in the air, and then fell once more.

Adelaide smiled and moved her hand slowly, forcing Atlanta to turn. "Watch!" she hissed.

Atlanta felt her mind instantly go blank at the sight of James and Ryan fighting. Ryan had shifted fully, his fur torn in places and his claws in James' back. James held a blade that was glowing a bright green and was holding Ryan down.

Stop! she tried to scream, but her voice was lost.

Ryan was pinned down, his claws piercing James' body. Still it seemed that James was a second away from killing the boy. Ryan's eyes were glowing red, and Atlanta knew instantly that he was being compelled.

She watched in horror as her uncle lifted the blade, ready to stab Ryan, and she wanted to scream at him to stop. She tried to force herself out of the spell she was under, but the more she tried the more agonizingly it held to her. She called out to her uncle and Ryan over and over in her mind, but her screams were whispers that wouldn't escape her lips.

She stared on in horror.

James brought his blade down as Atlanta screamed inside her head. She tried to close her eyes, but Adelaide forced her to watch. The seconds passed by in slow motion.

"Witch!" James screamed as he brought his blade down next to Ryan's head.

Ryan growled, trying to force James off, but the Druid was quick and brought the hilt of his blade across Ryan's jaw. Atlanta watched Ryan roll to the side, unconscious.

James turned to Adelaide, panting, his eyes glowing a similar green to hers, his teeth clenched in anger.

"Let her go," James hissed.

Adelaide let out a shrill laughter. "Druid, you surprise me," she cooed. "Why would I ever do that? I have plans for young Atlanta."

"It ends here, Adelaide," James hissed. "I'll kill you before you hurt her."

Adelaide's laughter died. "Son of Beatrice, you're already too late."

James let out a cry and charged, and before Atlanta could blink an eye, before she could even try to break free of her trance and stop him, Michael was there. Atlanta felt heat soar through her and she finally found her voice, screaming in renewed pain, scorched from the inside.

It was all the distraction that was needed.

James lost his focus, his eyes darting to her. For a brief second, Atlanta saw the emotions race through them. She saw the mix of worry, fear, love, and paternity. She saw every single minute of their life together mirrored in his eyes. The second lasted an eternity as her existence played out in a heart-wrenching kaleidoscope of images before her.

And then it was gone.

Time returned, and she watched helplessly as Michael wrapped his arms around James and thrust one clawed hand into her uncle's chest.

Atlanta's world shattered.

Darkness like she had never known descended on her. Her heart stopped, her breath caught, and her mind burst into fragments. She stared at her uncle's wide eyes in disbelief, unable to accept what she was seeing, yet helpless to turn away. James stared back at her, lifeless in Michael's arms before the hybrid dropped him to the ground.

She screamed.

She called out to James.

She thrashed and kicked.

She did everything she could possibly think of to break free from her frozen state and rush to James' side.

But all she could do, all Adelaide would allow her to do, was watch.

Michael turned to her, the smile on the hybrid's face wide as he licked her uncle's blood off his fingers.

Atlanta felt the world around her darken. Everything became a blur. *It's a nightmare. It has to be. This isn't happening.*

"Now, my dear, dear Atlanta," Adelaide whispered from behind her, laughing. "It's time we finish what I've been waiting so long for."

The last thing Atlanta registered before the darkness took over was her uncle's lifeless gaze.

Chapter 23

ATLANTA WOKE, LYING in the shadowy corners of the Dome. Her eyes took a moment to adjust, but when they did she instantly wished they hadn't. In front of her was the door. The door that so many had died to keep closed. Ravens were pinned to it with nails, their blood dripping onto the darkened floor.

She could hear whispers calling out her name in rhythm and echoing against one another. The candlelight was flickering and the darkness around her was being suddenly lit by even more candles that burst to life.

The voices behind the door kept calling her, and they grew louder as she began to stand. She felt like she was rising from a long and dormant death, every muscle in her body sore and heavy.

She felt compelled to wander around the Dome, but there was no exit from where she was. She walked along the path the candles made for her, down a long hall that seemed like an endless tunnel.

There were ravens dead and hung on the walls behind every candle. It seemed like a dark, ancient ritual had taken place there. Flashes of memory started to reach her conscious mind, and she recalled Adelaide.

She saw her forest-green eyes everywhere in the tunnel. They chased and haunted her wherever she went. Atlanta kept moving forward, oblivious as to where she was going or why. It was almost as if her body was magnetically drawn to something. She marched softly until she came across a series of candles laid out in a circle on the floor. There was something in the middle.

She hurried her pace, and as she neared it she stopped.

It's a body!

The body was on its back, the face hidden by a dark sheet stained in green and red. She leaned in to remove the sheet, and as she slid it off she realized who it was. She removed the sheet completely and let her tears fall like leaves off an autumn tree at the sight of James' pale face. His eyes were shut and his hair covered his forehead.

She fell on her knees and wept for what seemed like an eternity before she covered his face with the sheet again. "I'm so sorry," she said over and over, as if she could somehow bring him back. "I didn't know. I'm so sorry."

She reached out to hold his hand for one last time, and as her fingers slid in between his they scraped against something metallic. She pulled her hand back and held the brass key up to the candlelight.

The key was round at the top and equally wide at the bottom. Symbols were etched on both sides, a language she couldn't recognize but looked oddly familiar. She took the key and walked back towards the door, almost as if drawn to it.

The ravens on the wall suddenly croaked and awoke from their death. Terrified, Atlanta ran. The ravens chased her. She realized she was reliving her nightmare from weeks before. Her back hit the door, and she slid and fell to the floor. She screamed but there was no one around to hear it.

No one but the figure of Michael appearing from the shadows on her left, and Adelaide walking towards her from the path of candles in front of her.

At that moment, she realized that the fate of Calen was being decided.

What everyone feared would happen was on the verge of unfolding. She held the key tightly in her hand, but her senses told her that it was not the key that they needed. Michael and Adelaide stopped in front of her, their eyes glaring.

"Open the door." Adelaide's voice came in whispers from every corner of the room.

Atlanta's fears suddenly subsided, the ravens settled into silence, and the whispers from behind her began echoing Adelaide's words. Her deep-green eyes were the only sight that Atlanta could see. Their evergreen forced a stillness and calmness into her heart. Her uneasiness suddenly disappeared. She was not fighting anymore. The struggle ceased to exist. The whispers had become friendly voices and serene melodies, the call of friends beckoning.

A smile stretched across Adelaide's face. A light shone from the cracks of the door, and then many followed, seeping through as Atlanta turned to face it.

I should open this. I need to know what's behind it.

She felt excited and inexplicably drawn to the lights shining behind the door.

She held the brass key in one hand and took a deep breath. She pushed the key into a small rectangular hole right in the center of the door.

The stains of blood around the door turned into shades of green, and the whispers from behind it echoed the words, *"Come closer."*

Atlanta moved closer, not only drawn to the soft cries but feeling like she was one of them. The curls of green mist surrounded her, and a surge of wind came out the door.

She suddenly felt her heart twist around itself, and the euphoria that she had felt began to sink into an utter depression of the soul. She suddenly remembered the helpless look on James' face and the tear that fell from his eye right before he died. She remembered Ryan lying on the rooftop, worn out and drenched in blood. The darkness around her suddenly lifted, and she could see her surroundings clearly.

Adelaide and her hybrid were gone.

She looked at where the door was, and there was a desolate empti-ness behind it. It was dark and the candles couldn't even shed a speck of light into the room beyond. She looked behind her.

I opened the door! She stared in disbelief. *I let the hybrids out!*

She turned and ran towards her uncle's body but it had also disap-peared, the circle of candles surrounding nothing but emptiness.

She fell to her knees, her body shaking uncontrollably, and wept.

As she cried, the people of Calen woke to a new day, oblivious to the chaos she had brought down upon them.

THE END
Coven Master
Now Available – Excerpt included!

COVEN MASTER Blurb

THE CITY OF CALEN HAS fallen.

The forces that once held the city as one are scattered and drained of power. Adelaide, one of the witches who's haunted and threatened the peace once made by the elders in the territory, has regained her power by releasing the hybrids she's created. She's determined to destroy Calen and all those who stand in her way.

Atlanta, the Druid huntress, responsible for unlocking the hybrids and the murder of her uncle, tries to come to terms with what's happened. Determined to try and set the wrong right, she enlists the help of her kind, willing to risk everything, including her life, to stop Adelaide.

Suddenly she finds herself in a different town, fighting the witch and facing secrets about her past that leave her overwhelmed and vulnerable.

Meanwhile, Ryan and Marcus are in Calen, uncertain of what's happened to Atlanta and desperate to find her. They must face the hybrids over and over again, as the waves of power press down on them.

The fate of Calen rests in too few hands. Divided sanctions, Vamps, Wolf and Druid, must unify or each race stands no chance of survival.

NEVER LOOK BACK
    Coven Master
    Alpha's Permission
    Blood Bonding
    Oracle of Nightmares
    Shadows in the Night

Paranormal Huntress Series #2

Coven Master

EXCERPT

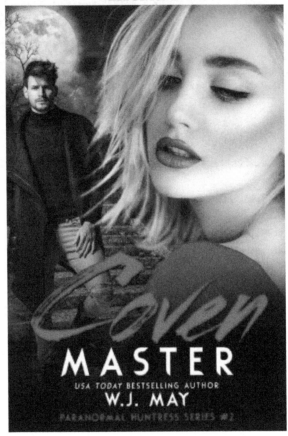

Chapter 1

A blaze of velvet red pierced the fine white sky. Silhouettes of birds and echoes of their morning song resounded in the air. They soared high, as if escaping some sullen malice that lay underneath. They formed an array of poetic welcoming for the rising of the sun in the broad and warm skies of the city of Lisbon.

The waves surrendered to the magnetic call of the shore's lips. The mountains behind spoke in silence as they were swallowed by grey skies. At the base of the mountains, on the other side from the shore, a slim figure strolled through the rocky steeps. His movement so silent that, even within the stillness that surrounded him, the echo of his footsteps was a mere whisper.

He walked with purpose, eyes set on a destination in front of him, unblinking as the winds curled and tossed around him.

The rocks on the mountain ahead of him were in shades of dark grey and reddish brown. He gazed at them for a moment from afar, then turned his head to a nearly twenty-foot-tall yellow rock formation to his right. He approached the rocks while constantly scanning his surroundings, making sure he wasn't being followed. He listened for the sound of footsteps or even the tremble of stones nearby. Nothing could be missed.

Satisfied that he was indeed alone, he knelt before the limestone rocks and reached out to a dirty greenish rock that sat alone, engulfed within the yellowness of the rocks. He pushed the rock into the wall.

In seconds, a passageway right behind the rock formation was revealed and he became swallowed inside it.

Surrounded by darkness he swiftly made his way down the narrow passageways, deeper into the mountain.

It didn't take him long to reach the end of his trek. He pressed his hand against a glass door and waited patiently until it slid open. Instantly bathed in fluorescent lights that shone whiter than snow, he blinked and let his eyes adjust. He walked in, through the tunnel of light, and down a second passageway much clearer than the first. His footsteps echoed as he picked up speed. His high black boots rang with the sounds of metal chains.

It was like a maze of tunnels bathed in brightness. He opened doors, turned left and right, and almost robotically moved toward a destination known only to him. The force with which he pushed the doors open gave the impression that the thin man was either quite angry or agitated. The shades of red on his forehead and the sweat running down his cheeks were both a sign of distress and the product of the endless walking he had to endure.

But even though his breathing was heavy and labored, he didn't stop to rest. For nearly thirty minutes he roamed the tunnels, pushing through one door after the other, driven by instinct and an obscure purpose known only to him.

He finally stopped at a hallway with three doors. He fixed his gaze on the one right across from him, marched towards it, then hesitated.

Wrong one.

He turned and pushed the bar on the door to his left and swiftly slipped inside.

There were mirrors on every wall and on the ceiling. The floor was adorned with a plush, bright-red rug. The room was hexagonal in shape and the lights inside burned a bluish white that made his eyes water. The floor and the bars that hung on every corner looked like those in the basement of the Skolars back in Calen.

The man finally took a moment to stop and catch his breath before walking towards the small brown door in between two mirrors.

He pressed his finger on a small round button to the right and waited. "It's Raul," he said.

Seconds later a buzzer sounded and the lock on the door released. Raul pushed the door open into a room similar to the one he'd just left. But, unlike the mirrors on every wall, this one gleamed with portraits and paintings in golden frames. Each painting depicted a man or a woman in crimson red or dark blue suit. The paintings were engraved with dates that went back centuries.

A round table in the middle of the room caught Raul's attention. Four people sat, two on each side, their attention drawn to a fifth man standing on his own. The conversations had stopped as everyone turned to look at the newcomer.

"Raul?"

Raul looked at the young man in charge of the meeting and swiftly made his way to him. "Sorry for interrupting," he said, the urgency in his voice grabbing everyone's attention. "I know it isn't my place, but I have some terribly important news."

Not that entering a hidden building and barging into a secret meeting wasn't important.

This, however, couldn't wait.

Raul didn't wait for a response. "It's about the city of Calen."

Chapter 2

Calen

Midnight was a glimpse away; the hours passed as if minutes

were dust that flew out of a broken hourglass. There were desolate shafts

of light that would peek into the streets, trying hard to shed themselves

over the darkened corners of the city, all in vain. The dust filled the air,

casting its shadow over the towers of Calen. If one would gaze at the

city from afar, they'd think that a sandstorm had caught the pillars of

every building with its rough claws.

Along with the darkness, there wasn't a single moment of silence. Not a second passed without the heavy sound of cracking, or confused screams, or the zapping of wires ripped out of their circuits. The city itself was crumbling, along with the people inside it.

In the suburbs, the Skolar house sat in ruins. Shingles were strewn about on either side of the house, and the grass looked as if it was reaching out to swallow the crushed skeleton of what remained of the house. Half the grass had yellowed from lack of sun, but oddly continued to grow. The other half had been scorched. Only the basement was the only part that laid untouched, unharmed by the constant hail of fire that fell from the gargoyles' breath onto the streets of Calen.

Further into the city, the majestic gothic structure of Calen High stood proud. Oddly, with minor damage done to it. As Adelaide's hybrids roamed the dust ridden corners of the city, Marcus waited inside.

We're all doomed.

Marcus stepped out of the principal's office, where he had spent the past few days regaining his strength. He stretched, letting his fangs elongate and retract, as if making sure they would still obey his will. He gazed down the dark, empty hallways, wondering how this could have happened.

It'd been nearly two weeks since the door had been opened.

By the end of the first day, it was no secret the hybrids were out. Adelaide made sure everyone—mortal or supernatural—knew her forces were taking over the city. Marcus remembered it clearly, as if it had happened just yesterday. He'd been in his thirteenth-floor office, surrounded by the best of his guards, when the heavy roaring of the wind first began to howl through the city. It was followed by the sound of shattering windows and the fusion of metals bombarding into one another.

Marcus had stepped out onto the terrace of his office, surrounded by a thick blanket of dust and wind that prevented him from seeing anything further than a few feet away. He had felt the grains scrape against his skin and eyes, threatening to engulf him, making sure Adelaide's hybrids could operate under its shroud unhindered.

He knew he could not be compelled by the hybrids, knew that the elders of the Vampire clan were immune to the beasts' trickery. Still, there was little they could do when they couldn't see, or sense, the enemy.

Adelaide had clearly been counting on that.

She's bloody planned every step. Been planning for years.

The memory still burned in the back of his mind. How he'd walked back into his office to find his guards dead. How the wind had howled all around him and red eyes had peeked through the clouds of dust surrounding him. They'd come for him, three of the beasts, eager to rid themselves of the threat Marcus posed to their dominance. They were a formidable force, but he had no intention of letting them win. In the end, he'd gotten the better of them. He could still feel their green hearts pounding in his palm before he crushed them.

If only we could've controlled them.

Marcus barked in laughter and shook his head. Even now, alone and without a plan, he was thinking of how he could use this attack to his advantage. The desire to be the dominant race, to be king of all, was etched in his every bone, and the fact that he was now prey to something even more superior bothered him tremendously.

The Druids. I need to find the Druids.

But even that idea seemed senseless. James was the last Druid, and he hadn't seen the man since the nightmare had started. Atlanta was missing, too. Marcus knew James was dead, but Atlanta... what had happened to her?

Not that I would know. I've been locked up in here for a fortnight.

Even though the hybrids had fallen, he had taken quite a beating. It had taken all his strength to storm out of the lair and find his way here, to hide in the shadows and regain his strength. His healing had taken time, more time than he was used to, and he knew it was because of the poison that coursed through Adelaide's hybrids.

He'd been frozen by her charms before.

An anger burned deep inside him as he walked down the empty corridors of Calen High. Every few steps, his eyes would catch the decaying corpse of a fallen human. He had fed on the ones still alive when he'd arrived.

Students torn to shreds, teachers gasping blood. They were going to die anyway, and he'd needed all the blood he could get to recover. Now their corpses looked like mangled pieces of flesh, the rot they emitted burning his sinuses.

We need to regroup.

Marcus scoffed at the thought. Regroup where? And how? He didn't even know if there was anyone alive who could fight alongside him. He knew he couldn't trust anyone other than the elders of his own group, yet he doubted even their survival. He was going to have to find out either way. They would need everyone able to fight against Adelaide and the hybrids.

Inside the nearly unmoving corridors, the whistling sound of water running down the broken dispensers barely muffled the screaming outside. The costume of the school mascot lay on the floor of the hallway, torn to pieces. Marcus walked on the ceramic floors that were tiled in blue and red squares, between open lockers with their hinges scattered around the floor. Pages torn from books were dust-ridden and flying about. He made his way to the back exit of the school.

It was nearly dusk outside, the crickets barely whispering as the football goalposts turned a pale shade of yellow. Marcus sprinted towards the posts, one after the other, testing his strength and making sure he was fully recovered before he could venture beyond the protection of Calen High.

I need to find the others.

Even though his centuries'-old pride whispered at the back of his mind that he alone could take down an empire of hybrids, he remembered he was also the reason this was happening. It was his blood that gave birth to the malice that encompassed the city.

It might not be directly, but he was responsible for everything.

He couldn't shake the thought that, without the Druids, they couldn't have stood a chance against the hybrids a century before. He remembered how the Werewolves had fought alongside the Druids in the insurgence, a massive force he'd marveled at. Back then, it had seemed like the Vampires were actually holding everyone down. Marcus scowled at the memory. They'd been so helpless back then.

As they were helpless now.

The level of humiliation Adelaide had thrown upon his race enraged him.

Never again.

He leapt from the tall football bleachers, frowning as his eyes glowed a bloody shade of red. His movements were swift as he dashed across the field and left the temporary haven of Calen High. He roamed every street and every rooftop of every tower in Calen. And as his feet pounded the concrete of the streets, his eyes could still see his own Vampires glaring at him as he ran. Some tried to reach for him, and he slashed through them as if they were paper, ripping them apart with a sickening ease he took no comfort in.

They're not mine anymore. They're compelled.

Marcus searched many places before finally reaching the three towers where James Skolar had been. The dust seemed less dense here, and the green of the forests behind him glowed in the morning sun. His eyes were met by the flickering of red light on top of one of the roofs, a little underneath from where the sun was shining.

He dashed into the building, and within seconds found himself crashing through the rooftop door. His feet crunched on the pebble-covered floor, his eyes catching sight of the destruction across the neighboring towers.

There's been a fight here.

The ground to his right had been carved with a body that was missing, and his keen eyesight caught droplets of caked blood on the pebbles around. There were stains of blood at the right corner of the roof, and he caught a whiff of something pungent, something dark.

From the corner of his eye, he caught movement.

Marcus turned quickly, immediately ready for a fight, fangs stretched and craving to sink themselves in flesh. A few yards away his eyes fell on a body, motionless except for the rise and fall of labored breathing.

Marcus relaxed, retracting his fangs as the harsh reality sunk in.

Ryan Toller.

Chapter 3

Darian's presence always demanded respect.

As the leader of The Coven, one could not deny the power that seemed to ooze from him wherever he went. His slightly broad shoulders and piercing pale-blue eyes demanded attention, and always seemed attentive and assertive. His light-brown hair was sparse on the sides and stood up on the top of his head. His sideburns reached just under his earlobes; his beard a mere shade over his angular cheekbones. He was young, but the knowledge he possessed was well beyond his years.

Before Raul had come in, Darian had gathered the eldest of the Druids in his region to discuss their interference with the conflict that had been raging in a small town in Armenia. The Vampires in the surrounding area had decided to assert their dominance and attacked, wiping out the entire town.

Darian, obviously distressed over the issue, felt a need to send some of the Druids over to investigate and resolve the problem. And, if necessary, remain there to protect the town. The leaders he was meeting with were mostly in agreement with everything he was suggesting. However, they were reluctant to go there themselves and the matter was too small to require all of them to attend to it.

Except Darian felt it a responsibility of his own to take even the most extreme measures to make sure the Vampires weren't harming, let alone killing people The Coven was meant to be protecting. He made it a point to use instances like this to make an example of those who fell out of line. It wasn't because of the responsibility of being the leader, which was to ensure the safety of the people, but more the nature of who Darian was. The combination of duty and the guilt had been passed down through the centuries, generation to generation, until it ran in his blood.

Although only twenty, what he lacked in experience he made up for in knowledge that could be sensed from merely looking in his eyes. Darian's wisdom exceeded that of men twice his age. The man knew how to think things through, and his insight to the others was never challenged—often—anymore. His young intelligence was incomprehensible to many.

When Raul walked in, Darian immediately noticed the drop of sweat sitting on the man's forehead. He could hear his friend's heavy breathing disguised in the controlled slow pace that Raul tried to maintain.

"Lost in the labyrinth again?" Darian asked, addressing his friend in a confident and comforting tone.

"My memory of those doors is rusty," Raul replied.

"Well, welcome back, friend!" Darian said, pointing to the chair across from him, signaling for Raul to sit down.

Raul gazed at the others and then back at Darian, his lips stretched in a slight smile. "Happy I'm back?"

"Your disappearance made me fear the worst," Darian responded.

"I'm still around." Raul smiled, but Darian didn't miss the exhaustion in his friend's eyes. "It was impossible... even miles around Calen, there was no way I could reach here. Our signals have been jammed."

Darian wasn't surprised. "All right, gentlemen, shall we continue this meeting another time? I'd like a private word with Raul, here."

The leaders left with displeased looks on their faces. It was no secret they despised the fact that a man much younger than they, for some even half their age, was calling and dismissing them, ordering and disordering them whenever he wanted. However, they knew better than to act on their discontent. Darian knew that. They all recognized the power he possessed, and knew that, because he was the descendant of the former Coven, he was the only one fit to lead them.

They left the room with Darian sitting across Raul. The formality dissipated the moment the door was closed and the friendship between the two showed. Darian got up and walked over to one of the paintings on his left, then slid it down from its frame. There was the classic safe behind the painting; however, this one didn't hide any gold, but a bottle of wine and glasses.

He brought the wine and sat closer to Raul. "A drink to celebrate your return, my friend."

"After what I've just seen, one bottle isn't going to be enough," Raul replied, his words followed with a sigh as he wiped the sweat off his forehead with the sleeve of his shirt.

Months before Darian had given Raul, a junior Druid, the task of tracking down the settlers in the west and mainly in America, to try to find out where the concentration of Vampires and Werewolves had settled. Raul had communicated with Darian many times during the long months of his journey. However, upon reaching Calen, all communication had been lost.

The elders who had sat around the table had never heard of the city of Calen. The despair in Raul's voice seemed unnecessary to all of them because the city was foreign. However, Darian knew Raul had come back to confirm what had troubled Darian's mind for years.

Darian was known to be a very patient man. Even after seeing the distress on Raul's face, he didn't ask for the news immediately. Rather, the two drank the wine and talked endlessly until Raul's face softened and the harshness eased. Darian didn't need to hear Raul's story before attempting to find a solution. Rather, every small expression on Raul's face was a sentence that spoke to him on its own, and in response Darian had already begun planning his next step. As Raul was rambled on, Darian's mind began working in a completely different direction.

"All right, friend, it's time," Darian said. Raul immediately straightened in his seat and pushed his empty glass away. "What happen in Calen?" Darian asked.

"Do you know James Skolar?" Raul replied.

"I've heard of the Skolars. They were the leaders of the American Druids a long time ago. What about him?"

"I found him when I reached Calen or, more specifically, he found me. Apparently, his is—was—the only remaining family of Druids there, and for the past century they've managed to live in complete harmony with both the Vampires and Werewolves."

"You said *was* the only family." Darian noted the look on Raul's face, and didn't like it. Something wasn't right.

"That's why I came rushing back," replied Raul. "James Skolar is dead. His niece, the only remaining Druid, is nowhere to be found." He sucked in a sharp breath. "and Calen is in ruins."

Darian's pale blue eyes grew paler. This was not good. There had been no warning of what might happen. No one had asked for help. Had there been no time? "What happened?"

Raul shook his head solemnly. "My friend, I was in the middle of it when it all happened. James told me about the insurgence that happened in Calen a century ago. He said the Werewolves were chained by the Vampires before the Druids arrived and set them free. However, between the two events, Adelaide the witch used the blood of the eldest Vampire, Marcus, to create a hybrid of both Vampire blood and wicked witchery. It—"

"Did you say Adelaide?" Darian interrupted.

"Yes, Adelaide."

Darian felt his hand ball into tight fists. "What happened in the insurgence? How did it end?"

"Adelaide escaped when the Druids captured and locked the hybrids behind a door they built in a place called the Dome. Now, after they've managed to keep it closed for more than a century, the door has been opened, and the hybrids are out in Calen." Raul continued talking about the story James had told him, but Darian's mind drifted elsewhere. His thoughts were fixated on Adelaide.

Finally, he thought. *I have found you at last, Adelaide.*

W.J. MAY

END OF EXCERPT

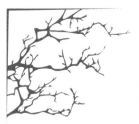

Find W.J. May

Website:
http://www.wanitamay.yolasite.com
Facebook:
https://www.facebook.com/pages/Author-WJ-May-FAN-PAGE/
141170442608149
Newsletter:
SIGN UP FOR W.J. May's Newsletter to find out about new releases, updates, cover
reveals and even freebies!
http://eepurl.com/97aYf

More books by W.J. May

THE CHRONICLES OF KERRIGAN

Book I - *Rae of Hope* is **FREE!**
Book II - *Dark Nebula*
Book III - *House of Cards*
Book IV - *Royal Tea*
Book V - *Under Fire*
Book VI - *End in Sight*
Book VII – *Hidden Darkness*
Book VIII – *Twisted Together*
Book IX – *Mark of Fate*
Book X – *Strength & Power*
Book XI – *Last One Standing*
BOOK XII – *Rae of Light*

PREQUEL –
Christmas Before the Magic
Question the Darkness
Into the Darkness
Fight the Darkness
Alone the Darkness
Lost the Darkness

Hidden Secrets Saga:
Download Seventh Mark For FREE

LIKE MOST TEENAGERS, Rouge is trying to figure out who she is and what she wants to be. With little knowledge about her past, she has questions but has never tried to find the answers. Everything changes when she befriends a strangely intoxicating family. Siblings Grace and Michael, appear to have secrets which seem connected to Rouge. Her hunch is confirmed when a horrible incident occurs at an outdoor party. Rouge may be the only one who can find the answer.

An ancient journal, a Sioghra necklace and a special mark force life-altering decisions for a girl who grew up unprepared to fight for her life or others.

All secrets have a cost and Rouge's determination to find the truth can only lead to trouble...or something even more sinister.

RADIUM HALOS - THE SENSELESS SERIES

Book 1 is FREE:

Everyone needs to be a hero at one point in their life.

The small town of Elliot Lake will never be the same again.

Caught in a sudden thunderstorm, Zoe, a high school senior from Elliot Lake, and five of her friends take shelter in an abandoned uranium mine. Over the next few days, Zoe's hearing sharpens drastically, beyond what any normal human being can detect. She tells her friends, only to learn that four others have an increased sense as well. Only Kieran, the new boy from Scotland, isn't affected.

Fashioning themselves into superheroes, the group tries to stop the strange occurrences happening in their little town. Muggings, break-ins, disappearances, and murder begin to hit too close to home. It leads the team to think someone knows about their secret - someone who wants them all dead.

An incredulous group of heroes. A traitor in the midst. Some dreams are written in blood.

Courage Runs Red
The Blood Red Series
Book 1 is FREE

What if courage was your only option?

When Kallie lands a college interview with the city's new hot-shot police officer, she has no idea everything in her life is about to change. The detective is young, handsome and seems to have an unnatural ability to stop the increasing local crime rate. Detective Liam's particular interest in Kallie sends her heart and head stumbling over each other.

When a raging blood feud between vampires spills into her home, Kallie gets caught in the middle. Torn between love and family loyalty she must find the courage to fight what she fears the most and possibly risk everything, even if it means dying for those she loves.

Daughter of Darkness - VICTORIA
Only Death Could Stop Her Now
The Daughters of Darkness is a series of female heroines who may or may not know each other, but all have the same father, Vlad Montour.
Victoria is a Hunter Vampire

Don't miss out!

Visit the website below and you can sign up to receive emails whenever W.J. May publishes a new book. There's no charge and no obligation.

https://books2read.com/r/B-A-SSF-NMSN

BOOKS 2 READ

Connecting independent readers to independent writers.

Did you love *Never Look Back*? Then you should read *Only the Beginning*[1] by W.J. May!

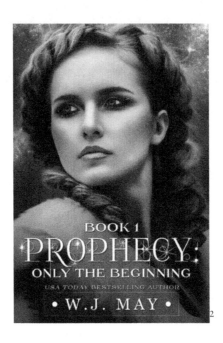

USA TODAY Bestselling author, W.J. May brings you the highly antici-pated continuation of the Hidden Secrets Saga. The Twisted Red Riding Hood fairytale continues in the Prophecy Series. This is a stand alone se-ries, or maybe be read in continuation of the Seventh Mark books.

Be Prepared. There are werewolves in this story, and they are NOT friendly.

Peace comes at a price...

Rebekah and Jamie are happy, but discontent. Sometimes, it feels like everything important has already happened, that the peace their parents fought so hard to bring them is just a strange limbo they can't break out of. They want adventure, they want to make memories of

---

1. https://books2read.com/u/31gZdl

2. https://books2read.com/u/31gZdl

their own. When a pair of new kids show up at their school, it looks like they might finally have their chance.

It isn't long before the twins open up to the mysterious new strangers. Sharing secrets they thought they'd never tell. Asking questions they never could have imagined.

When a party in the woods leads to near tragedy, they find themselves caught in the middle of a fight they never saw coming. Trapped between two sides and put to the ultimate test.

Will they choose their family? Or their future?

Rogue's adventure may have come to an end, but the twins is just getting started...

<u>PROPHECY SERIES</u>
In the Beginning
White Winter
Secrets of Destiny
<u>HIDDEN SECRETS SAGA</u>
Seventh Mark - Part 1
Seventh Mark - Part 2
Marked by Destiny
Compelled
Fate's Intervention
Chosen Three
Read more at www.wjmaybooks.com.

Also by W.J. May

Great Temptation Series
The Devil's Footsteps
Heaven's Command
Mortals Surrender

Hidden Secrets Saga
Seventh Mark - Part 1
Seventh Mark - Part 2
Marked By Destiny
Compelled
Fate's Intervention
Chosen Three
The Hidden Secrets Saga: The Complete Series

Kerrigan Chronicles
Stopping Time
A Passage of Time
Ticking Clock
Secrets in Time
Time in the City
Ultimate Future
Guilt Of My Past

Mending Magic Series
Lost Souls
Illusion of Power

Challenging the Dark
Castle of Power
Limits of Magic
Protectors of Light

Omega Queen Series
Discipline
Bravery
Courage
Conquer
Strength
Validation
Approval
Blessing

Paranormal Huntress Series
Never Look Back
Coven Master
Alpha's Permission
Blood Bonding
Oracle of Nightmares
Shadows in the Night
Paranormal Huntress BOX SET

Prophecy Series
Only the Beginning
White Winter
Secrets of Destiny

Revamped Series
Hidden
Banished
Converted

Royal Factions
The Price For Peace
The Cost for Surviving
The Punishment For Deception
Faking Perfection
The Most Cherished
The Strength to Endure

The Chronicles of Kerrigan
Rae of Hope
Dark Nebula
House of Cards
Royal Tea
Under Fire
End in Sight
Hidden Darkness
Twisted Together
Mark of Fate
Strength & Power
Last One Standing
Rae of Light
The Chronicles of Kerrigan Box Set Books # 1 - 6

The Chronicles of Kerrigan: Gabriel
Living in the Past
Present For Today
Staring at the Future

The Chronicles of Kerrigan Prequel
Christmas Before the Magic
Question the Darkness
Into the Darkness
Fight the Darkness
Alone in the Darkness
Lost in Darkness
The Chronicles of Kerrigan Prequel Series Books #1-3

The Chronicles of Kerrigan Sequel
A Matter of Time
Time Piece
Second Chance
Glitch in Time
Our Time
Precious Time

The Hidden Secrets Saga
Seventh Mark (part 1 & 2)

The Kerrigan Kids

School of Potential
Myths & Magic
Kith & Kin
Playing With Power
Line of Ancestry
Descent of Hope
Illusion of Shadows
Frozen by the Future

The Queen's Alpha Series

Eternal
Everlasting
Unceasing
Evermore
Forever
Boundless
Prophecy
Protected
Foretelling
Revelation
Betrayal
Resolved
The Queen's Alpha Box Set

The Senseless Series

Radium Halos - Part 1
Radium Halos - Part 2

Nonsense

Perception

The Senseless - Box Set Books #1-4

Standalone

Shadow of Doubt (Part 1 & 2)

Five Shades of Fantasy

Zwarte Nevel

Shadow of Doubt - Part 1

Shadow of Doubt - Part 2

Four and a Half Shades of Fantasy

Dream Fighter

What Creeps in the Night

Forest of the Forbidden

Arcane Forest: A Fantasy Anthology

The First Fantasy Box Set

Watch for more at www.wjmaybooks.com.

Made in the USA
Las Vegas, NV
03 March 2021